D0961532

Life, After

SARAH DARER LITTMAN

SCHOLASTIC PRESS
NEW YORK

Library of Congress Cataloging-in-Publication Data

Littman, Sarah.
Life, after / by Sarah Darer Littman. — 1st ed.
p. cm.
Summary: When poverty forces her family to leave their home in Buenos Aires, Argentina, Dani has a hard time adjusting to life in New York, where everything is different except her father's anger, but she forms an unlikely bond with a wealthy girl at school that helps heal both of their families.

[1. Immigrants — Fiction. 2. Moving, Household — Fiction. 3. High schools — Fiction. 4. Schools — Fiction. 5. Jews — United States — Fiction. 6. Hispanic Americans — Fiction. 7. New York (N.Y.) — Fiction. 8. Argentina — Fiction.] I. Title.
PZ7.L7369Lif 2010
[Fic] — dc22
2009020523

ISBN 978-0-545-15144-3

10 9 8 7 6 5 4 3 2 1   10 11 12 13 14

Printed in the U.S.A.   23
First edition, July 2010

The text type was set in Sabon.
Book design by Becky Terhune.

To Claudette Greene, for trusting me to write this book, and in memory of victims of terrorism worldwide.

Chapter One

NORMAL KIDS WERE HAPPY when the bell rang at the end of the school day. Normal kids couldn't wait to escape from the boring science lecture given by Profesor Guzmán, who had been teaching at the Escuela Hebrea Maimónides since before the television was invented. Normal kids packed up their books, then went to fetch their uniform blazers, chattering all the while with their friends.

But I wasn't a normal kid, because I preferred to listen to Profesor Guzmán's ·interminable lecture rather than go home.

I knew I would have to leave eventually. But I tried to put off the moment as long as I possibly could, waiting until the classroom was empty except for me and Profesor Guzmán, who slid a sheaf of test papers into his battered leather briefcase with wrinkled, liver-spotted hands.

"Did you have a question for me, Señorita Bensimon?" he asked in his quavery voice.

"No . . . I was just thinking. . . ."

Thinking, and trying to ignore the chorus of hungry growls from my stomach.

"Well, I'm afraid I'm going to have to ask you to think outside, because I need to lock the classroom," he said.

Why Profesor Guzmán was so compulsive about locking his classroom door every night had been a topic of speculation at our school for years. Gaby was convinced he was hiding something sinister in his desk, but I always thought it was because he was afraid someone would steal his precious skeleton, Señor Moshe, to whom he seemed to have an abnormal attachment.

With a sigh, I gathered my books and shoved them in my bag. I hoped that Roberto didn't have to stay late so we could walk together, and maybe take a detour to the park. Anything to put off the moment when I had to go through the door to my family's apartment.

I didn't always feel that way. There was a time, Before, when I too was a normal girl who looked forward to the end of the school day, looked forward to going home where Mamá would be waiting with tea and *alfajores*, my favorite cookies, always there to help with my homework if I needed it.

That all changed in 2001, because of the Crisis. It's amazing how quickly life can change for the worse. I mean, it wasn't like a war started with bombs dropping or guns firing. But first the government instituted the *corralito*, which restricted the amount of money people could withdraw from their bank accounts. That prompted the *cacerolazos*, where people marched in the streets banging on pots and pans because they were so angry they couldn't use their own money. Sometimes the protests got violent, with rioters breaking the plate glass windows of banks and tearing down billboards of foreign companies like Coca-Cola.

This eventually brought down the president, Fernando de La Rúa, who had to be flown away from the presidential mansion, Casa Rosada, by helicopter because it was too violent outside in the Plaza de Mayo. Then we had a crazy period where there were three different presidents in three weeks, finally ending up with Eduardo Duhalde. He made the decision to let the peso float against the U.S. dollar, and within a month our currency lost eighty percent of its value. Practically overnight, people like my father went from comfortably middle class to poor. Papá's customers couldn't afford to pay him, so he couldn't afford to pay his suppliers. He struggled to keep things going, but in the end he had to close the clothing store. Fortunately, Mamá, who was a nurse before she had me, was able to get shift work at a local hospital, so we weren't completely destitute. But still, it seemed like we lived in a country where every day the floor was sinking a little farther under our feet.

I walked down the empty hallway and into the school courtyard, where students stood clustered around the jacaranda tree waiting for their parents to pick them up, or gossiping before starting the walk home. Just six months before, my best friend in the world, Gabriela Tanenbaum, would have been waiting for me under the jacaranda's canopy of purple flowers, tossing her red curls as she flirted with Leo Alvarez. We would have walked home together, talking without pausing for breath, but maybe stopping for *helado*, chocolate for me and *dulce de leche* for her, not that it really mattered because we always shared.

I suppose Gaby still *is* my best friend in the world, except now she lives on the other side of it — yet another example of how the Crisis turned my world upside down. Her family emigrated to Israel a few months after the peso crashed and things went from bad to worse. They decided to take advantage of the great benefits the Israeli government was offering to Argentinean Jews to make aliyah to the Promised Land.

The ranks of our school thinned as more families moved abroad or couldn't afford the tuition, even with scholarships from Jewish organizations like the Asociación Mutual Israelita Argentina and the Joint Distribution Committee. I wouldn't have still been there otherwise. One of the draws of going to a Jewish day school was supposed to be small class sizes, but if the Crisis went on much longer, they would be microscopic.

"*Hola*, Dani!"

I turned with a smile to greet my *novio*, Roberto.

"How was Guzmán?" he asked.

"A real snoozefest, as usual. I don't know why they don't make him retire."

"*Es cierto*. Guzmán was ancient when my father had him." He smiled at me, and, as always, I felt like there were butterflies fluttering in my chest. "So, do you have time to walk home through the park today?"

There was a glint in his brown eyes that I knew meant a stop under the ombú tree, where a year before, nestled against its twisted trunk and shaded by the massive canopy of leaves, we shared our first kiss. A glint that told me that although I knew I should go straight home to make sure Papá was okay like Mamá asked me to, I was going to walk to Parque Los Andes with Roberto. Anything to stall going back to the apartment, where a perpetual storm cloud seemed to loom overhead.

"*Vamos*," I said. We left the school grounds walking shoulder to shoulder, close enough that we bumped arms as we walked past the concrete security barriers that protected the gates of our school ever since the terrorist attack on the AMIA building in 1994. After that, barriers and guard huts were set up outside of every Jewish institution in Buenos Aires. They became a perpetual reminder of how life could end in an instant.

Roberto waited to take my hand until we turned the corner, out of sight of the school grounds; then he raised my hand to his lips and kissed it.

It was warm for a November day in late spring. Roberto's kiss made me feel even warmer.

"Did you hear about what happened to my parents' friends, the Medinas?" Roberto said.

"No. Tell me."

"My mother was hysterical about it this morning at breakfast. Someone broke into their house and robbed them the other night."

"Was anyone hurt?"

He put his arm around me, a strong, protective band of warmth.

"Not badly. But the robbers roughed up Señor Medina and tied up him and his wife. One of the neighbors noticed the front door was left open the next morning and found them."

"I can't believe it. Don't they live in Belgrano? That's a nice area. . . . You'd think they'd be safe there."

Roberto sighed and his arm tightened around my shoulders.

"When over half the people in the country are going hungry, nowhere is safe anymore, Dani. People are desperate."

Desperation was a feeling I knew well. Anxiety about my family's situation was a wolf gnawing at my insides, every minute of every day. Well, except for the time I spent with Roberto under the ombú tree, when he would kiss me into forgetfulness.

"Ricardo Levi told me his family is going to Israel," Roberto said. "They're leaving in two weeks."

"*¿De verdad?*" I sighed. "So many people have gone already. Sometimes I feel like all our friends are leaving and soon we'll be the only ones left."

"I know what you mean, *amor*," Roberto said. We reached the gate at the entrance to the park and started heading down the path toward the bench near our tree. "But you wouldn't believe what Ricardo was saying. Apparently his family is getting all this money for making aliyah to Israel — something like twenty thousand U.S. dollars for moving and housing costs. It's almost like they get paid for moving there."

"That's why Gaby's family moved there." Maybe it was my mood, but I couldn't help thinking the worst. "Mamá heard a man on the bus saying all these bad things about Jews, like why are we getting paid money to leave the country, when ordinary Argentineans aren't getting enough help. It scared me. What if people start to —"

"Stop, Dani, you'll make yourself crazy worrying."

We reached the bench under the ombú tree and I threw my book bag down and sat next to Roberto. He put his arm around me and I felt his lips in my hair and on my forehead.

"In fact, if you keep on like this, you might make me crazy, too, and you wouldn't want to do that now, would you?" he said with a tender smile.

"*Make* you crazy, Beto?" I joked, using his nickname. "You already *are* crazy!"

"*Ay* . . . now you've done it," Roberto said, reaching his finger for the spot on my side where he knew I was super ticklish.

We wrestled for a few minutes until he finally caught me in a hug, and I rested my head on his shoulder.

I couldn't help thinking about how wonderful it would be if my family were suddenly handed a check for twenty thousand U.S. dollars just because we stepped on a plane and left this place, where life seemed to grow more difficult by the day.

But then I looked around me at the familiar park, at the proud line of tipa trees and the purple blooms of the jacarandas. I could hear the hum of traffic on Avenida Corrientes, "the street that never sleeps," where in better times, when Papá still owned the clothing store, he used to take Mamá out on Saturday nights for dinner and the tango. I glanced up at Beto's handsome face and thought, *How could I leave all of this?* Buenos Aires was my home, where I'd lived all my life. Yes, things were difficult, but times had been hard before. My parents used to speak in hushed tones about the "Dirty War" during the 1970s, when thirty thousand people were "Disappeared" without a trace if the government didn't like them, like Mamá's cousin Enrique, who was a student at the Universidad de Buenos Aires. His parents made the rounds of all the police stations and government agencies, but no one would tell them anything. Many years later, after the military government fell, they were told that Enrique had been drugged like a zombie and then pushed from a military cargo plane into the Atlantic Ocean. But they had no body, no real proof of what had happened to him — nothing to mourn.

People say that Argentina is a country that lives with ghosts. But it was my home.

"Would you ever want to leave?" I asked Roberto.

He didn't answer right away, and I felt cold suddenly, even though the sun was shining.

"I don't know," he said. "I mean, I've always wanted to study in another country. We talked about doing that while we're in university."

I smiled. "Yes, Paris, London, New York — so many choices. How will we ever decide?" I let out a heavy sigh. "Not that my parents are going to be able to send me anywhere, if things stay the way they are."

"I know," Beto said, shaking his head. "Who knows if we'll be able to afford any of our dreams now? But, Dani, I always planned that if I did go away to study, I would come back here afterward. It's where my family and friends live. It's where *you* are."

He brushed away a strand of hair from my cheek.

"The thing is, *amor*, if things keep going downhill like this, I don't know how anyone will be able to survive here."

Roberto must have seen the panic in my eyes, because he kissed me, gently, on the lips before he continued.

"I know you're scared, Dani. I'm scared, too. Every night my mother nags my father about moving to America, to Miami, where my *tío* Tico lives. But Papá doesn't want to leave his medical practice because in America he would have to retake his exams to be certified as a doctor."

I stroked the dark curls at the back of his neck, wishing I could say or do something to comfort him. But I was thinking about the scene at home last night. Mamá said that she was going to the soup kitchen at Beit Jabad to get food, because she couldn't sleep knowing that Sarita and I were hungry. Papá was silent at first, and I thought maybe he'd recognized we'd reached the point of desperation. I should have realized that it was a dangerous quiet, the quiet before the explosion of a rage so loud and ferocious that Sarita ran and cowered behind me. I wished I had someone to hide behind.

"*We will not take charity!*" he shouted. "*I would rather starve!*"

"Daniela, take Sarita to your room," Mamá said in a low, uneven voice.

I didn't need to be told twice. Sarita and I huddled together on my bed and I tried to read her a story, but all the time I was trembling and thinking, *Well, fine if you want to starve, but why make us starve along with you?* It seemed so unfair that Papá would make the decision for all of us, when I knew in my heart — and my stomach — that it was the wrong one. I could hear Mamá and Papá arguing, even though the door was closed; Papá louder, Mamá quieter, but arguing all the same. I wondered if there were any happy houses left in Buenos Aires.

"The thing is, I know we're better off than a lot of people right now," Beto was saying. "Still . . . a lot of Papá's patients can't pay him because they can't afford to. But he can't just stop treating them."

He stood suddenly and started pacing back and forth.

"I'm so sick of this, Dani! I want to be able to take you out on a real date, to the cinema, to a café, not just to a park bench. I wish . . ."

Roberto sat back down next to me, his shoulders slumped over, his head in his hands. "I just want this to be over and life to be back to normal again."

I sighed, and rested my head on his shoulder. "I know, Beto. Even if I don't remember what normal feels like anymore. All I know is that at least under the ombú tree with you, I'm happy."

"Me too," Roberto said. "And I'd be even happier if you'd kiss me again."

I laughed and made him happier.

Eventually, I had to head home. Roberto said he would walk me most of the way before he caught the bus back to his house. We left the haven of the park for the commotion of Avenida Corrientes. Holding hands, we walked by an empty storefront where there used to be a bookstore, past the boutique where I could no longer afford to shop, and, worst of all, across the open doorway of the *parrilla* where the smell of steak cooking nearly brought me to tears. I couldn't remember the last time I'd had a thick, juicy steak, the kind Buenos Aires was famous for, but I dreamed of them on a regular basis.

Even though the economy had caused some businesses to close, there were still enough restaurants and pizzerias open to make the walk down Corrientes tortuous, so I pulled Roberto down one of the cross streets, Gurruchaga, which was quieter and more residential.

"When this is over and we have money and we're old enough to travel together, where should we take our first trip?" I asked him. We did a lot of fantasizing; except back then I still thought of it as planning our future.

"What about America — Cali-for-ni-a?" Roberto said, speaking English and putting on a really terrible American accent. "We should go to Hollywood, *baby*! Because you are going to be a *star*!"

I was laughing and posing like Marilyn Monroe when I saw something that made me grab Roberto's arm and drag him behind a transit van. He misunderstood, ducking his head to kiss me, but I pushed him away and peeked out from behind the van at a sight I couldn't believe — my father coming out of the Parroquia Santa Clara de Asís, the local parish church, carrying a bag of groceries. My father, who only the night before had shouted at my mother that he would rather we all starve than accept handouts.

I felt hot and cold at the same time, a feeling twisting in my gut that was part hunger, always the hunger, but part something else, which I couldn't identify.

"What is it, Dani? What's the matter?"

I watched my father round the corner before turning to look at Beto's concerned face.

Should I tell him? I wondered. After all, he was my *novio*; shouldn't I have been able to tell him anything? Wasn't that what Mamá had said to Papá — that he shouldn't be ashamed of being poor, that so many other people like us were in the same situation because of the Crisis and that at least we weren't living in a *villa mísera*, or shantytown . . . at least yet.

But it was no good. I guess I was too much like Papá, because I *was* ashamed of being poor. I hated that our lives had changed so much, so quickly. Only a year and a half before, my life had felt secure. My father owned a clothing store that his grandparents started. We lived in a small but comfortable two-bedroom apartment in the middle class neighborhood of Villa Crespo. I had a great group of friends and could afford to go out to the café with them once in a while with the money I earned for babysitting my younger sister when my parents went out to dinner. But our entire existence Before was built on a fragile foundation of suddenly worthless pesos.

I loved Roberto, and I trusted him. But even though I knew things were hard for his family, too, Dr. Saban wasn't sitting at home all day being angry and depressed about life. I didn't want Roberto to know that things had gotten so bad at my house that we'd had omelets every night for dinner the last week, and that sometimes I woke up with drool on my pillow because I'd been dreaming about steak and chocolate and *alfajores*. But most of all, I didn't want Roberto to know that my proud *papá* was begging for food at the church.

"It's nothing."

I gave Roberto a kiss on the lips to prove it, then took his hand and dragged him back onto the sidewalk, under the shade of a plane tree. He was still looking at me with furrowed brows. Beto knew me too well for me to be able to pretend things were okay the way I could with everyone else.

"What about New York?" I said, trying to distract him. "I've always wanted to go to Broadway. We could see shows and walk in Central Park — oh, but maybe you've had enough of walking in parks. We could go to museums and art galleries and maybe a baseball game and . . ."

Roberto put his finger on my lips to quiet my frantic chatter.

"Dani, tell me. What is it? What's the matter?"

His warm brown eyes met mine with love and concern. Part of me wanted to tell him. But I just couldn't. Something stopped me . . . shame, pride, whatever you want to call it; I just couldn't let him know how far my family had fallen. It was hard enough to accept it myself.

I felt my eyes fill, and dropped my gaze to the pavement.

"I've got to go — Papá . . . Sarita . . . I . . ."

I stood on tiptoe to give him a quick peck on the cheek, then ran away down the street, my book bag thumping against my thigh, ignoring Beto's calls for me to stop, to come back.

A block away from our apartment I did stop, but only to catch my breath and use my sleeve to wipe away the tears that streamed down my cheeks and dripped from my chin. I couldn't let my father see me in such a state, because he would have asked me why, and I would have had to tell him that I saw him begging from the Christians, and then there would have been shouting and who knows, maybe that would have been the time that he raised his hand as well as his voice; maybe that would have been the time that he hit me.

If you'd told me a few years ago that I might someday be standing a block away from my apartment, afraid to go in because I'd be scared my father might hit me, I would have laughed. Or said you were crazy. I might even have gotten mad at you for thinking something so ridiculously absurd about my kind, gentle, and loving *papá*, so mad that maybe we might not be friends today.

But you would have been right and I would have been wrong. Because that was Before, and everything was different then.

When I let myself into the apartment, Papá was sitting in front of the television, watching the news with the blinds closed, which made the apartment even more gloomy and oppressive.

"There's a letter for you," he grunted. "It's on the kitchen table, with the rest of the mail."

His eyes didn't leave the TV set, but I was thankful about that, for once.

The thin blue airmail letter was waiting for me on the table, amidst all the bills, bills, and more bills. It was postmarked Israel, and I recognized Gaby's sloppy scrawl. There was also a letter from America, from Tío Jacobo. I wondered why Papá hadn't opened it, but was too anxious to read my own letter to think much about it. It was the first letter I'd had from Gaby since she'd left. I threw my book bag on the floor and carefully slit open Gaby's letter with a kitchen knife.

Sometimes, when I thought about the suicide bombers

blowing themselves up in Israeli pizzerias and discos, I wondered if Gaby and her family were so lucky to get away from here. I wondered how it must feel to go to a café or the mall and worry if the person next to you was wearing a vest of explosives under their jacket, waiting to kill you — and themselves.

But then, where was safe? After watching the Twin Towers fall in New York City on September 11 the year before, it was hard to know if anywhere was free from danger: Buenos Aires, Jerusalem, New York, London, Paris, Rome — or any of the other places Beto and I dreamed of visiting someday.

I slid into one of the kitchen chairs and started to read:

Dear Dani,

I'm really sorry I haven't answered any of your letters before now. Will you forgive me? It's just been crazy trying to settle in and learn Hebrew and adjust to a new country. It's so weird living on the opposite hemisphere from you — I can't believe it's autumn here and spring there! I miss you SOOOOOOOO much! How are things? We hear such terrible stories about what's going on in Argentina — businesses closing left and right, Jews living in shantytowns, imagine!

My Hebrew is finally getting better. Who would have thought all those years of struggling with it at the Jewish day school would pay off? We're living in an absorption center in Ra'anana, which is about 19 km north of Tel Aviv. Every day I have to attend ulpanim, which are intensive Hebrew classes for immigrants like us. There are quite a few people from Argentina here — also lots of Americans, British, and South Africans. Señora Owen would be pleased that I'm getting a chance to practice my English.

In a way it's kind of unreal, like living at a big summer camp except with your parents there, too. There are lots of kids my age — some cute guys, I might add ☺ — and in the evenings we go down to the lounge and hang out together or walk down to the city center. We're supposed to practice our Hebrew all the time, but English seems to be the common language for a lot of people. Or we end up speaking "Heblish," a mixture of Hebrew and English and whatever other languages are spoken by the people in the group.

It's going to be strange in a few weeks when we have to move out of here into our own apartment somewhere. You're only allowed to stay in the absorption center for six months and then you're considered to be assimilated enough to be let loose into normal Israeli society. That scares me. I like it here at the Ra'anana center because we're in Israel but in this place we're all extranjeros; no one is going to laugh at me if I make a stupid mistake when speaking Hebrew or forget how to make change in shekels when buying a coffee. Maybe *that's why "the authorities" kick us out — they don't want us all sticking together in our little immigrant ghetto — even if it's a nice ghetto with classes and cultural events and parties.*

I miss you, Dani. How are things with you and Roberto? Is he still your novio? *I worry when I hear about how things are back home. I hope things are okay for you and your family. Give Sarita a hug for me. And write back — SOON!!!!!! Gaby*

I could hear Gaby's voice in my head as I read, and I missed her so much my chest ached and my eyes burned with tears that I would not allow myself to shed. Not there. Not then. Not with my father brooding on the sofa in the next room and my mother and Sarita due home any minute.

Instead, my stomach rumbling, I opened the refrigerator to see what I could start for dinner. I found some vegetables that Papá must have received from the church. There was a new box of pasta on the shelf, some bags of dried beans, and a big bag of rice that hadn't been there when I left for school. It would make a pleasant change from omelets.

But all the time I was wondering, *What should I tell Mamá?* After Papá said he'd rather let us all starve than take charity from the Jewish organizations, how could I tell her that I saw him taking food from a church?

My tummy didn't care whether the food came from a Christian charity or a Jewish one. My tummy only cared that there was enough to stop the constant pangs of hunger.

Mamá would notice the extra food, though. She fought to stretch every practically worthless peso to make sure we stayed fed and clothed. She would surely notice the extra pasta and rice and vegetables. How would Papá explain it?

I decided to brave the uncertainty of his mood and ask him myself before Mamá came home.

"Papá?"

"Yes, Dani?"

"I saw there's some extra food in the kitchen."

Papá slowly pulled his eyes away from the television and muted the sound. His face contorted slightly and then he actually . . . smiled. A strange, awkward, uncomfortable smile, but still . . . I hadn't seen a smile on his face in weeks.

"You'll never guess what happened this morning, Dani. I was able to get some day work today . . . helping to unload trucks at the supermarket. I happened to be walking there and they were shorthanded — and, well, with the money I was able to buy some extra groceries."

He's lying. For the first time in my life, I was consciously aware of my father looking me in the eye and telling me something that I knew to be untrue. I didn't know how to react. How could he lie to me like that? Why would he tell me such a blatant falsehood? I felt an angry denial welling inside me, *No, Papá, I saw you coming out of the church with a bag of groceries,* but seeing my father's uncertain eyes and pained smile, the words caught in my throat.

I took a deep breath and put an equally fake smile on my own face. How could I blame Papá for lying about taking charity when I couldn't even tell Roberto the truth? If he had his pride, well, so did I.

"That's wonderful, Papá! Mamá will be thrilled. And so will Sarita. I'm going to make pasta tonight, so we won't have to hear Sari complaining about having omelets again."

"That sounds delicious, Dani. I . . ."

"What is it, Papá?" I asked.

"It's nothing. I only wish we had a nice Malbec to go with it. It's been a long time since your mother and I shared a bottle of wine over dinner."

He had a sad, wistful look on his face and I suddenly got a glimpse of my old *papá* from underneath the unpredictable, moody mask I'd been seeing, the kind and loving Papá I knew from Before. It filled me with such a longing that even though I was angry with him for lying to me, I couldn't stop myself from going over and giving him a hug.

"Things will get better soon, won't they, Papá?" I asked, my face buried in his shoulder.

I could hear the slow *whoosh* of air from his lungs as he let out a deep sigh and wrapped his arms around me, hesitantly, as if he, too, were no longer sure where we stood with each other.

"Every day I pray it will be so, Dani."

He didn't sound like he expected his prayers to be answered.

I wanted to tell him that praying wasn't enough — that he had to pull himself together and go to one of the job centers. But I didn't want to risk the rare feeling of closeness to my father, even if it was all based on lies.

I cleaned some vegetables and put water in a pot for the pasta, then sat at the kitchen table to do my homework. But as much as I tried, I couldn't concentrate on memorizing cell structures. It wasn't the hunger, although that was there, as always, nagging away at the corner of every thought. It was just that every time I tried to focus on the purpose of the Golgi apparatus, images of my "Before Papá" kept floating into my brain — like the times before Sarita was born when we would walk together, hand in hand, to the end of the long wooden pier by the Club de Pescadores to watch the fishermen trying their luck in the Río de la Plata. Papá was always good at starting conversations back then; inevitably he'd make friends with one of the fishermen, so the man would let me touch the cold scales of the fish in his buckets, or even "help" him fish by putting my little hands on the rod. "Before Papá" had crinkles around his eyes, but from laughter, not anger; that father told funny stories that he made up himself, and made Mamá and me laugh with his constant jokes.

How could that Papá have turned into the person who now sat in the living room — one who alternated between gloomy silence and raging anger? A man who would lie to his family just to save his pride? It was as if the wonderful shiny perfection of my Before father's image had cracked to reveal this unpredictable, imperfect stranger.

Should I tell my mother the truth about the food? Hadn't my parents always taught me it was wrong to lie?

The words of the science notes blurred — *Golgi apparatus: organelle found near the cell nucleus, processes and packages macromolecules (mainly proteins and lipids) for secretion* — as my eyes filled with tears. As much as I missed having a full stomach, I missed having my real father more.

Chapter Two

ON MONDAY JULY 18, 1994, I turned seven years old. On that same day, Tía Sara, my father's sister, was killed, along with eighty-four others, when a truck bomb ripped apart the AMIA building at 633 Pasteur Street. She was eight months pregnant with a baby girl, who would have been my cousin.

At the time, I didn't understand how the event would change my life. I was just upset and angry that everyone was crying on my birthday, because to my seven-year-old mind, birthdays were inextricably linked with laughter and fun, with parties, games, presents, and, best of all, cake. To make matters worse, Mamá called all my friends' mothers to cancel my birthday party, so I didn't get to wear the beautiful new dress with blue ribbons and shiny patent leather shoes that Papá brought home from his clothing store especially for the occasion.

Instead, Mamá and I spent the day sitting by the telephone, hoping that Papá would call with news from Pasteur

Street, where he and Tío Jacobo were waiting in unendurable agony, praying that by some miracle Tía Sara was alive. Every time I left the room, Mamá would turn on the television, switching it off as soon as I came back in, but sometimes not before I'd caught a glimpse of the gaping wreckage of the building where Tía Sara worked. What had been normal and safe suddenly looked ugly and terrifying, like an open wound on the flesh of the city.

When they finally pulled Tía Sara's body from the rubble, all hope was lost — and my *papá* was a changed man.

I remember when he got back from Pasteur Street. He sat hunched over in his chair, reeking of smoke, his clothes caked with dust.

"Papá? Are you okay?" I asked him, worried.

He lifted his head, and even though I was only seven at the time, I will never forget the agony I saw etched on his dirt-streaked features. Papá picked me up and held me tightly on his lap, so tight it was almost painful. He buried his face in my neck and burst into wracking sobs.

"She's gone . . . Dani . . . my sister . . . gone. *D-os mío . . . why?*"

I'd never seen my father cry before, and his despair frightened me so much that I started crying, too. He held me like he would never let go; the stubble on his unshaven chin scratched my cheek.

I was relieved when Mamá came in and released me from Papá's grasp. She spoke to him quietly so I couldn't hear, and then gently suggested he go take a bath and change his clothes. Papá didn't even seem aware that he was dirty or that the smell of burning building clung to him, but he followed Mamá's instructions like a child.

While he was in the bathroom, Mamá covered the mirrors with sheets, the way Jewish people do in a house of mourning. It scared me when I walked into the living room early the following morning in the dim half-light — I thought there was a ghost coming through the wall and ran screaming into my parents' room.

I didn't go to school when it started again the week after the bombing because we were in mourning for Tía Sara. Her funeral was my first ever. The coffin, a simple pine box with a Star of David etched into it, seemed too small to contain someone as bighearted and wonderful as my *tía* Sara.

"Do you think Tía Sara is afraid, all alone in that box?" I whispered to Mamá, who sat between Papá and me. Papá was trying to comfort my *abuela* Debora, whose eyes were red and swollen from crying. My *abuelo* Oscar stared straight ahead, as still as a museum statue.

"No, *querida*. I think G-d is keeping her company."

I thought about that for a minute, then whispered again into my mother's ear, "But it's only a small box. It must be crowded with both of them in there."

My mother smiled and hugged me tight, but I saw myself reflected in her eyes, which glistened with tears.

The worst part, though, was the cemetery. I hadn't really understood that they were going to put Tía Sara in a hole in the ground and then cover her up with dirt. When they finished saying all the prayers, the rabbi handed Tío Jacobo a shovel. With tears streaming down his handsome face, he slid some dirt from the pile next to the hole onto the back of the shovel and then, with visibly shaking hands, tossed the dirt into the grave. It landed on Tía Sara's coffin with a loud *thud*, and I felt Mamá shudder. Tío Jacobo handed the shovel to my *abuelo*, who repeated the action, and then to Papá, who threw some dirt, then handed it on to someone else. I couldn't understand why everyone would do this to poor Tía Sara and I started crying hysterically, *"Mamá, Mamá, stop them . . . Tía Sara . . . is . . . alone . . . dark . . ."*

Mamá carried me from the grave site to a bench not far away. She sat me on her lap and held me, stroking my hair until I calmed down.

"Dani, Tía Sara's soul is with G-d now. It's only her body that remains in the coffin, and her body isn't afraid. The body is just a vessel. . . ."

"What's a vessel?" I sniffed.

"It's like a container, *querida*. A container for the part of her that made her the person we knew and loved, loved so very much."

"So she's not afraid of the dark under all that dirt?"

"No, *amorcita*," Mamá said, kissing my damp cheek. "Where Tía Sara is now, there is only light."

Three days after the bombing, on Thursday, July 21, my mother took me with her to a protest march from the wreckage on Pasteur Street to the Plaza de los Dos Congresos. We walked in silence, and then stood for hours in the rain under a sea of umbrellas with two hundred thousand others, to show our shock, our sadness, and our anger. I was cold and my feet hurt, but I tried not to complain — at least, not too much — because Tía Sara was dead, so many others were dead, and I didn't want to give Mamá any more reasons to be sad.

But that didn't stop me from having nightmares for weeks afterward. Nightmares of monsters with jagged claws like the broken beams of the destroyed building. Nightmares of being trapped alive beneath mountains of rubble, calling out for help and not being heard. I would wake up struggling beneath my blankets, sweaty and crying.

I wasn't the only one. Papá barely slept at all, he was so tormented by visions of what he'd seen during his vigil at Pasteur Street. He was pale and gaunt, and he never smiled. The change in him frightened me almost as much as the monsters in my dreams.

Then, about five months later, Mamá got pregnant and gradually, as her belly swelled, Papá's fog began to lift. He still wasn't the same Papá as Before — life would never be the same as before July 18, 1994 — but when Sarita was born and named in memory of my aunt, right from the beginning she was so noisy and vibrant that she forced everyone to focus on the living. It was as if she were saying, *I'm here! Look at ME!*

And things were better, for a while. Until the Crisis happened and life as I knew it changed forever.

"Dani, what kind of cake is your favorite?"

I was half-asleep when Sarita asked the question — there was light coming in from behind the curtains, but I was sure it wasn't yet time to get up for school.

"Chocolate, of course. What time is it?"

"Five thirty. Why 'of course'? I like chocolate, but I also like Mamá's lemon cake with the poppy seeds."

"Sari, it's five thirty in the morning," I said, rolling over to look at her. "Why on earth are you waking me up to talk about cake? Go back to sleep!"

I could barely make out her face in the faint dawn light, but I heard the tremor in her voice.

"I can't sleep, Dani. I'm hungry. My tummy keeps making growly noises like a bear."

A stabbing sensation in my heart joined the perpetual pang of hunger in my stomach. I lifted up my blanket.

"Oh, Sarita," I said. "Come here and have a cuddle."

Sari climbed into my bed and I curled myself around her small, warm body. I rubbed her tummy, as if that could make the hunger go away.

"Things will get better soon, Sari. I know they will."

I knew nothing of the sort. Our country was in free fall, like when the roller coaster suddenly goes down a steep incline, leaving your stomach at the top of the slope.

Shivering, even though it wasn't cold, I curled closer to Sarita, drawing comfort from her warmth as I crooned one of her favorite nursery rhymes:

"*Arroz con leche, me quiero casar, con una señorita de San Nicolás, que sepa bordar, que sepa tejer, que sepa abrir la puerta para ir a jugar. Con ésta sí, con ésta no, con ésta señorita me caso yo.* . . . Rice pudding, I want to marry, a lady from San Nicholas, who knows how to embroider, who knows how to knit, who knows how to open the door to go play. With this one yes, with this one no, with this one I'll be wed."

Sari's breathing slowed as she fell back to sleep, but I lay awake until it was time to get up for school, thinking about chocolate cake.

Time passes more slowly in school when you're hungry. The second hand on the clock seemed to move in slow motion. Sometimes I could have sworn it moved backward. I wish. If only I could have turned back time, I would have moved it backward to Before. Papá would be happy and

Tía Sara would still be alive. There wouldn't be an economic crisis and Gaby would still be in Buenos Aires. We'd meet every day after school and walk home together, stopping for ice cream because we could afford it.

"Daniela, I asked you a question," Señora Owen said, breaking into my fantasies of Life, Before.

"I'm sorry, what was that?"

"You were obviously miles away," she said in English. "It's an expression that means you were daydreaming."

Years away would be more accurate.

"Please, can you use the word *probably* in a sentence?"

I had to think for a moment about what the word meant.

"Um . . . *Probably* the Crisis will end soon, but most of the time it doesn't feel that way."

Señora Owen gave me a pitying look.

"Very good, Daniela. And I'm sure we all know how you feel."

Did everyone *really* know? I wondered. Sofia Mendoza told me that her aunt and uncle lost their home and had to move in with them and they had ten people living in a two-bedroom apartment. We didn't have that, but was her father too ashamed to take a charity box from a synagogue? Ricardo Levi's family decided to immigrate to Israel — but did his father lose a business that had been in his family for three generations? I knew that Mili Varela and I both ate the free lunches provided by the Joint Distribution

Committee, but did she too go to sleep dreaming of food, and have nightmares of waking up to find her family living in a *villa mísera*?

I knew I wasn't the only one suffering from the Crisis, but why did I still feel so incredibly alone?

Roberto was waiting for me at the school gate. I got the usual tingles in my stomach when I saw him. Although he smiled when he saw me, he looked uncharacteristically tense, his face pale and drawn. I worried, suddenly, that he was angry with me for running off yesterday without saying good-bye.

"*Buenas tardes*, Señor Velázquez," I called out to the security guard, who sat reading the *Página/12* in the hut beside the gate, his antiquated electric fan ruffling the edges of the paper with its faint, asthmatic current of air.

"*Buenas tardes*, Señorita Daniela," he mumbled back without taking his eyes off the page.

"Do you have to go straight home?" Roberto asked. "Or can you stop at the park for a while?"

"Sarita is going home with a friend, so I don't have to be home for at least an hour."

"Good. Let's go to the park."

I didn't tell Roberto that Mamá asked me to come straight home after school to keep an eye on Papá. I didn't want him to know that Papá was . . . the way he was. That ever since he lost the business in March, he had gradually withdrawn into himself, as if someone had turned off a light with a dimmer switch. That he spent a lot of the day sleeping, instead of going out and looking for a job.

I needed my time in the park. Those stolen moments with Roberto were precious to me. At the time, they felt like all I had.

Once we'd turned the corner and the school building was out of sight, Roberto took my hand in his. It was cold and clammy, despite the warmth of the late November spring sun. Beto was always such a good listener, but as I chatted to him nervously about my day at school, it was clear he was distracted.

When we reached our bench, I slung my book bag on the grass and sat, expecting Roberto to sit beside me. He put his backpack down, but he remained standing.

"Dani, I have to tell you something . . . something important."

A knot formed in my stomach. *He's going to break up with me. . . .*

Even before he opened his mouth to tell me the news, I felt the tears coming. Ever since Gaby and her family had made aliyah earlier that year, Beto had been more than my *novio*; he'd been my closest friend.

"My father . . . well, you know how hard things are right now . . . and well . . . my family — we're moving to America. To Miami. My *tío* Tico . . ."

Strangely, my initial reaction was relief — relief that he

wasn't breaking up with me. But then it hit me that he was leaving. . . .

"No," I whispered. "Not you, too."

Roberto sat and put his arm around me. I turned my face into his shirt and sobbed.

"But it was only a month ago you said your *papá* didn't want to leave. . . . Please don't go. Don't leave me."

I felt his lips against my hair as he hugged me.

"Dani, I don't *want* to leave you. I don't want to leave Argentina. It's my country — my home. My friends are here, you're here."

He grinned. "And River Plate, my favorite football team, is here. How am I supposed to leave? Americans don't take football nearly as seriously as we do. They don't even call it football! Soccer . . . what is *that*?"

I managed to giggle through my tears.

"Then stay. . . ."

"I can't, *mi amor*," Beto said, the grin wiped off his face. "You know that. I have to go with my family. My father can't make a living here anymore."

"I *hate* the Crisis! It's taking everyone away from me! First Gaby, now you . . ."

"I hate it, too, Dani."

I lifted my head and met his eyes, and was surprised to see they were glistening with unshed tears. My own tears had left a round, wet patch on his shirt.

"Sometimes I wonder if there will be anyone left here besides me," I sniffed. "It feels like everyone I love is leaving."

Roberto reached into his backpack and handed me a tissue. We sat under the tree where we held hands for the first time, where he kissed me for the first time. So many firsts. And soon . . . lasts.

"When . . . when will you go?" I asked.

"In December . . . when school ends."

So soon . . .

"I'll miss you, Dani. So much it hurts."

"What day do you leave?"

"The twenty-sixth."

I counted the days in my head. Thirty-six more days together and then . . . loneliness. Not even those moments in the park with Roberto to look forward to, those small oases of happiness in my desert of grim reality.

"I bet the girls in Miami are really pretty . . . blond and thin like in all the TV shows."

He hugged me closer.

"I'll be too busy missing you to notice."

I wanted so much to believe him.

We sat there holding each other for a little while longer before I looked at my watch and realized I had to get home.

Hand in hand, we walked in the warm sun down the noisy sidewalks of Avenida Corrientes. On the corner of

Serrano, a *cartonero* was rummaging through the garbage, stirring up the sickly sweet smell of rot as he looked for recyclables to sell, the trailer attached to his bicycle half-filled with cardboard and white computer paper.

"It's strange to see a *cartonero* out in the daytime," I said. "Usually it's nighttime before all the garbage pickers come out."

"Maybe he's trying to get ahead," Beto said as we turned to walk in the leafy shade of a quieter side street. "There are more *cartoneros* than ever because of the Crisis. I don't know how any of them can make a living."

At least they're trying, I thought.

"That's one thing about Buenos Aires I won't miss," Roberto said. "Seeing people picking through the rubbish every day."

"What, you don't think there are poor people in America? You think that everyone there is rich and happy?"

I knew I sounded bitter and angry, but I couldn't stop the words from leaving my mouth.

Beto looked at me reproachfully.

"Of course not, Dani. You know me better than that."

I did. I just didn't want him to escape and leave me behind.

"I'm sorry, Beto. I just . . ."

"It's okay, Dani. I know."

We walked together down the cobbled street, holding hands, until we got to my building.

"See you tomorrow, Dani," Roberto said, giving my palm a gentle squeeze. I wouldn't let him kiss me in front of our building since Papá started spending his days moping at home, in case my father happened to look out the window. But Beto's brown eyes gave my face a final caress before he turned away.

I watched him walk down the street until he turned the corner, postponing the moment when I had to open the door to our apartment. But then he was gone and I had no more excuses not to go inside. There were letters in the mailbox downstairs — my first clue about Papá's mood. He obviously hadn't made it out of the apartment. It looked like a Morose Papá Day.

When I looked through the letters, I felt pretty morose myself. Bills. All bills. Well, except for another letter from America, from Tío Jacobo. I was tempted to rip it open and read it, but I was afraid that could be tinder to ignite my father's temper. We never knew what would set him off. So I tucked it back in among the bills and slowly climbed the stairs to our apartment.

All was quiet when I opened the door. I assumed Papá was asleep, either in the chair in the living room or in his bedroom, so I tiptoed into the kitchen and tried not to make too much noise as I took out my books and started my homework.

I wrote my history essay and started on my algebra homework, but I found the word problems really confusing, even when my stomach wasn't growling from hunger and my calculations of the speed traveled by buses A and B weren't constantly being interrupted by the thought that Beto was leaving. Before, I could have asked Papá to help me, but not now. . . .

Halfway through I became completely stuck, so I gave up and started to peel potatoes for dinner. My mother was always so tired after work. It was so unfair that when Papá worked, Mamá always had dinner ready for him when he got home, but now that Mamá was working and Papá wasn't, he didn't do the same thing for her.

Mamá and Sarita came home just as I was finishing the potatoes. As usual, my seven-year-old sister bounced through the door, babbling away as if there weren't a sleeping ogre of a father nearby that I'd been tiptoeing around, trying not to wake.

"Dani, guess what! That mean boy in my class I've been telling you about is moving to Israel, so he won't be here anymore to pull my hair!"

"*Shhh!* You'll wake Papá!"

Mamá frowned. "He's still asleep?"

I nodded. "He's been asleep since I got home."

Mamá sighed.

"So, Dani, aren't you glad that Franco is moving? I am, because he's such a big meany and nobody likes him. Well, I mean, *some* people do but not me or Alicia or Rachel or Rafaela."

When Mamá was pregnant with my little sister, she used to complain how the baby was never still, and nothing has changed since. As Sari spoke, she hopped from one foot to the other, rattling the clean breakfast dishes that I left drying on the rack that morning before I went to school. I couldn't believe my father could sleep through all the noise.

Unfortunately, he couldn't.

"Sarita!" he bellowed from the bedroom. "Will you never be quiet? Stop that infernal chattering."

My sister jumped, her blue eyes huge and wide, as she realized she'd woken the sleeping monster. I glanced over at Mamá; she looked pained and tired.

"Come, Sari," I said. "Let's go read a story in our room."

Mamá mouthed a silent "thank you" and headed toward the bedroom to try to placate Papá.

Sarita cuddled up to me as we sat on her bed. She clutched her Baba, a ragged scrap of the blanket she was given as an infant, and stroked the edge of it between her thumb and forefinger.

"I wish Papá would move to Israel with the mean boy," she said.

"Shh! You shouldn't say that!"

"Why not? He's mean, too. He always yells at us. And he never smiles."

I realized that being so much younger, Sarita didn't have

the treasure chest of memories I had of the way Papá was Before. She didn't remember how he used to throw me up in the air and catch me, laughing and smiling; when he used to take us to the clothing store and show us off to the people who worked and shopped there; how he'd let me sit in the big leather chair behind his desk and pretend that I was the one in charge. As far as Sarita was concerned, Papá had always been the way he was: angry, unpredictable, and bitter. My heart twisted in my chest to think that this was the only father she remembered.

"He wasn't always like this," I told her. "Don't you remember four years ago, before everything got terrible, how we went on vacation to Mar del Plata for a week, and they had a sand castle building competition for kids, and Papá helped us build the biggest and best sand castle ever?"

Sarita wrinkled her nose and I saw a flicker of memory in her eyes. "You mean the one that looked like a fairy princess lived there? And I helped get the shells and the seaweed to decorate it?"

"That's the one. And remember how Papá always got us an ice cream, even though Mamá said it would spoil our appetite for dinner, because he said that ice cream belonged with the beach like he belonged with Mamá?"

Sarita giggled. "And then we'd have to close our eyes because they'd make kissy-face and it was yucky."

I smiled. "That's right. So you see, Sari, Papá wasn't always the way he is now. It's just . . . the Crisis. It changed him."

"I hate the Crisis," Sarita said, serious suddenly. "And I hate our Now Papá. I wish I could live here with just you and Mamá."

I can't deny that there were times I wished for the same thing, but the only way that would happen was if my parents got divorced, which I would have hated, or if Papá died, which I would have hated even more.

"Hush, Sari. Remember, it says in the Ten Commandments that you should honor your father and mother."

"Even if your father is mean and shouts at you all the time?"

"Yes, Sari . . . even then."

"Why? Why do I have to honor him if he's mean to me? *It's not fair!*"

I didn't know how to answer her — I hadn't had any expectation of fairness ever since that birthday morning in 1994 when everything changed because of a terrorist's bomb.

Because it wasn't fair that Tía Sara and my baby cousin died, or any of the other people. It wasn't fair that my best friend Gaby and her family moved to Israel, or that my boyfriend Roberto was moving to America. It wasn't fair that I was going to be stuck in Argentina with my moody father and my worried mother. It wasn't fair that my little sister was looking up at me expectantly with her huge blue eyes, waiting for me to reassure her that everything would be okay and that life was always fair in the end. Because even though she was just a little kid, I couldn't lie to her about something that important.

"I guess . . . some things aren't fair. They just . . . are."

Sarita's lower lip trembled and she hid her face in my shoulder.

"I don't like it, Dani."

I stroked her curls, fighting the tears that threatened.

"Neither do I, Sari. Neither do I."

When Mamá finally called us for dinner, Papá was already sitting at the head of the table. He hadn't shaved and his hair was tousled like he just got out of bed.

Mamá made an omelet using the potatoes I'd peeled and some bruised, tired-looking vegetables she'd picked up for cheap at the market.

"Not again," whined Sarita. "We had omelets three times already this week."

I kicked her under the table, warning her to hush, just as Papá's fist crashed down on the table.

"*¡Silencio!*" he shouted.

Sarita paled and shrank into herself, as if by becoming smaller she might escape from Papá's wrath. I hated to see her become less of her cheerful, chatterbox self. But we had learned how to tiptoe around my father's moods to preserve the fragile stability of our home.

"When I was your age we ate what my mother put on the table without complaint," Papá said. "And we finished every last bite of it, or we had to eat it at the next meal."

And Before, you always used to complain about that, I thought. *You used to tell me the story like my* abuela *was crazy for doing that to you.*

"Eduardo," Mamá soothed. "Come, eat your omelet. I even put in extra onions just the way you like it."

I wondered if Papá could hear the strain in her voice, the anxiety as she tried to calm him so he'd stop berating Sarita for being what she was — a child. I know that I could, and I told her so with my eyes. We'd learned to say a lot with our eyes since Papá became . . . like he was. Because when he was in one of his moods, many things were better left unsaid.

As I ate, I fantasized about opening my mouth and telling my father everything I was feeling. Telling him how much I hated him when he shouted at my little sister; how I hated the person he'd become since Tía Sara died, since the Crisis. Telling him how I hated that he didn't get out of bed and shower and shave, and that I was scared that if he didn't get out of his funk and help Mamá make money, we'd end up living in a *villa mísera*. Because I knew that even "nice Jewish families" like us had been forced to live in the shantytowns that were springing up on the edge of town and beneath highway underpasses.

I wished for the courage to say these things to my father, but couldn't bring myself to utter the words because if I said them out loud, they would become truth, puncturing the illusion that he was still the *papá* he once was. Instead, I sat there silently like the rest of my family, eating my dinner.

I told Mamá that I'd wash the dishes after I helped Sari get ready for bed.

"That way you can read Sarita her bedtime story."

And rest a little bit . . .

But Mamá read the unspoken words on my face.

"*Gracias, preciosa,*" she said. "My feet are killing me today. These wretched bunions are acting up again."

"Go put your feet up on the stool," I told her. "Or better yet, lie down on Sarita's bed."

Mamá sighed heavily as she stroked an errant lock of my hair back into place. I looked at her face and noticed new wrinkles around her tired blue eyes and threads of gray in her chestnut hair.

"You're a good girl, Dani. I know this must be hard for you."

She doesn't even know the half of it, I thought. I opened my mouth to tell her about Roberto, but just as quickly I shut it, trapping the words inside. I couldn't dump this on her when she was so exhausted. Maybe later. Maybe the next morning. *Maybe never . . .*

"Go rest, Mamá."

I was standing at the sink finishing the dinner dishes when Mamá came back into the kitchen after reading Sarita her story. She picked up a dish towel and started to dry the clean pots I'd left on the draining board. Papá was in the living room watching the news. I wished he wouldn't because the news was never good; all it did was make him more depressed.

"Why isn't Papá getting better? Can't the doctors give him something so he isn't like this anymore? You're a nurse. Can't *you* do something?" I asked Mamá.

I was angry with myself the minute the words left my mouth, because we all tiptoed around what ailed Papá as if there were some unspoken rule that we should never actually name it.

Mamá pursed her lips. I'd crossed a line, forcing her to confront the elephant in the room.

"It's very complicated, Dani. Your father is a grown man. I can't force him to take medication." She sighed. "He's suffered so many losses. Tía Sara, his parents, and now the business. It's been devastating for him. He feels like a failure."

"But Papá worked so hard! He tried everything he could

to keep the business going so that people could keep their jobs. It's not his fault that the government made such a mess of things. How can he think he's a failure?"

Mamá put her hand on my cheek.

"Dani, I'm not saying it's true. But it's how he feels. And it hurts his pride terribly to think of taking charity; he's used to being the one who *gives* charity."

She gave a bitter chuckle.

"When I think of how righteous and superior I felt every time we gave *tzedakah*; how I'd search the synagogue bulletin to see who gave more or less than Papá and me, like it was some kind of . . . I don't know . . . some sort of barometer of our social status . . . well . . . sometimes I wonder if this is G-d's punishment for my pride. To show me how awful it feels to have to rely on others for even the most basic needs."

I was shocked to see tears streaming down Mamá's cheeks. The last time I remembered seeing her cry was at Tía Sara's funeral.

"To rely on others . . . to feed my own children," Mamá sobbed. "I would never have thought it was possible. We've lived through such hard times; the dictatorship . . . the Disappearances . . . the bombings . . . and we survived, but to have to go to the soup kitchen for food . . . I think this is more than I can bear."

It scared me to see my mother cry like that. It was bad enough that my father didn't get out of bed most days. But to see my mother sobbing at the kitchen table, her face covered by her hands, her nails ragged instead of manicured and painted with bright red polish the way they always used to be — that, more than anything, brought home to me how bad things really were for us, and it scared me, scared me more than anything. I knew the situation was dire, but maybe the worst of the worst was lurking just beneath the surface, waiting to rip a hole in the frail vessel that held our family together.

I wanted my old *papá* back. I wanted him to sing "*Aishes Chayil*" to Mamá in his deep baritone on Shabbat, praising her for being a woman of worth. I wanted him to smile again, a genuine smile, not one to cover up a lie. I wanted him to be my father, instead of a stranger who didn't know me anymore. I wanted things to be like they were Before. I wanted my old life back.

But I couldn't tell my mother any of these things, despite the fact that I felt like crying myself. My mother had the weight of our entire family resting on her slim shoulders, which were hunched over as she sobbed silently into the dish towel. How could I add to the burden? So I swallowed the bitter taste of the lump that caught in my throat, and put my arm around Mamá to try to comfort her, wondering if there would ever again be a time when I could go back to being a normal girl with two normal parents living a so-called normal life.

Chapter Three

I HEARD MY PARENTS ARGUING as I was lying in bed. Sarita was sleeping soundly. I got out of bed and crept to the door, opening it a crack so I could hear what they were fighting about.

"Eduardo, Jacobo's right. It's the only thing that makes sense."

"No, Estela. I won't leave like the others. I've lived in Buenos Aires all my life. I'm a *porteño* through and through."

Leave? Leave to go where? America?

"Think of the girls," Mamá pleaded. "I can't bear to see them going hungry every day. It breaks my heart when Sarita complains about her tummy growling like a bear, and Dani . . . well, Dani doesn't complain, but I know she suffers."

"The girls will survive. We all will. We survived the Dirty War, we survived the terrorist bombings, and we will survive this, too."

"But don't you want more for your children than for them to merely *survive*, Eduardo? Don't you want them to be able to *live*? To live and be *happy*?"

"Who knows what it is to be happy, Estela? My sister, Sara, was happy. Then she went to work one day and never came home."

"You let the terrorists win when you think that way," Mamá said. "We owe it to Sara not to be defeatist, to fight so that our girls have every chance to live a good life. And Jacobo is offering this to us, by sponsoring us for a visa. How can you turn him down?"

Tío Jacobo. That must mean America, I thought. Where did he live again? Somewhere in New York, I seemed to remember. I wondered how far that was from Miami, from where Beto would be living.

"I can turn him down because I'm not going to be like all the others and run away from everything that means something to me just because times are difficult."

There was a silence that seemed to last an eternity.

"And the girls? Daniela and Sarita? What about me, Eduardo? Don't we mean anything to you?"

Mamá's voice broke on this last question, and then I heard her sobbing. I felt like crying, too. I wanted to go back to bed, bury my face in the pillow, and weep. But I needed to hear Papá's answer.

"Estela . . . come now, don't be ridiculous."

"Don't tell me I'm being ridiculous!" Mamá said, her

voice raised, but not shouting, clearly trying not to wake us. "What am I supposed to think? How I am supposed to feel? You mope around, getting more angry and depressed each day, but refusing to get treatment. You get angry if I try to get help from the Jewish community to feed our children — *our children*, Eduardo — and now, when Jacobo is offering a lifeline out of this dreadful situation, you refuse?"

Papá let out a deep breath. "Estela, you know that you and the girls mean everything to me.... You are all that I have."

"All the more reason to go to America, to give the children a chance. Who knows what kind of future they face here in Argentina?"

"Who knows what kind of future they'll face in America?" Papá argued. "At least in Argentina, everything is familiar, the culture, the surroundings, the language. We have friends and your brother and his children are still here, even if they are in Córdoba."

"That's true. But in America, we have Jacobo, who is family, too. And there, it will be better for the girls," Mamá said. "America is the land of opportunity."

"Yes, and the sidewalks are paved with gold," Papá mocked. "But let me tell you something, Estela. The sidewalks in America are made with cement, just like they are here."

"Don't speak to me like I'm an idiot, Eduardo," Mamá said, her voice edgy with exasperation. "I know that America isn't a magical Promised Land, where our problems will disappear. But at least we won't face constant political upheavals and economic instability, so there's a better likelihood that we'll be able to get back on our feet."

Even from my eavesdropping spot behind the bedroom door, I could hear Papá's weary sigh.

"I'll sleep on it, Estela. I'm not promising you anything other than that I will think about it."

I could hear my mother kissing my father. *¡Puaj!* Some things are better not seen or heard.

"That's enough for now, Eduardo. But think hard."

I crept back to bed and lay awake, staring into the darkness, contemplating the thought of leaving everything I had ever known. What had been a fantasy when I was walking home from the park with Roberto could become a reality. Who would have thought that a simple blue air letter with a U.S. postmark could carry such huge implications?

Mamá had to wake me up the next morning because I slept through the alarm.

"Were you up late reading?" she asked when I came into the kitchen for breakfast.

"No, Mamá." I wanted to ask her about Tío Jacobo's letter — to know if we might really move to America and if so, when, and did she really think that it would make our lives better. But that would mean admitting that I'd been eavesdropping on her argument with Papá, so I swallowed my questions along with my tea and slice of toast.

"You know the Sabans — Roberto's family — they're moving to Miami as soon as school ends," I told her.

Mamá was wiping the counter but she turned to look at me and then came to sit at the table.

"That must be hard for you, Dani," she said, taking my hand.

I nodded. "It seems like everyone is leaving Argentina, doesn't it? I mean, the Tenenbaums went to Israel, now the Sabans are going to America. . . . Lots of other kids at school have left."

I hoped that if I brought up all the others leaving, Mamá might talk.

"I know. That's how I got work at the hospital, because so many other nurses had emigrated." She shook her head slowly. "It's this crazy economic situation, Dani. It's like nothing that ever happened before in this country. I don't know where it's all going to end. Do you know, the other day at the hospital we had over thirty injuries from a *cacerolazo* that turned violent? One of them was an eighty-year-old man who was cut by flying glass when someone threw a rock through the window of a foreign bank. Imagine. What is this country coming to?"

She sighed and stood up, grabbing the dishrag.

"Believe me, as much as I love Argentina, I'd be on the next plane out of here if I thought it would give you and Sarita the opportunity for a better life."

"But how do you know that going somewhere else would *be* a better life?"

I knew I sounded just like Papá, but like him, I was unsure of the unknown.

Mamá laughed bitterly.

"It certainly can't get much worse than this, can it?"

I thought about the endless stack of bills, and my fear of losing our apartment and having to live on the streets. I thought it probably could get worse, but I didn't say this to Mamá. Some things were better left unsaid.

"Well, I'd better get to school while there are still enough of us left to hold classes," I said.

Mamá came and kissed my forehead. "Don't worry, Dani. Everything will be okay."

Her mouth said the words, but her eyes didn't look like she believed them.

"I think we might be moving to America, too," I told Roberto at lunch.

"Seriously? Where to?" He laughed and gave me a warm look with his chocolaty eyes. "Wouldn't it be fantastic if you were in Miami, too?"

"It would, but if we move, it would be to New York, where my *tío* Jacobo lives. How far is that from Miami?"

"I'm not sure, exactly, but far enough," he said. "It's definitely a plane trip or a very long car ride."

My heart sank. I only had a vague impression of the geography of the east coast of the United States, but I was hoping that Miami and New York weren't that far apart.

"Cheer up, Dani," Roberto said. "At least we'd be on the same continent."

I didn't have time to go to the park with Beto after school, because Mamá was working late and I had to pick up Sarita. When we got home, the apartment was dark and quiet. Papá wasn't watching television, which meant he was in the bedroom, sleeping. It was clearly another Morose Papá Day. I warned Sarita to be as quiet as a mouse and went into the kitchen to make us both a cup of tea. But when I flicked the light switch, nothing happened. I tried again, as if that would magically cause illumination to happen. It didn't. Magic was distinctly lacking in my life in those days.

I didn't know what to do. Did I risk waking up Papá to get him to check the circuit breaker? There was enough light to see, but not enough to do homework.

"What's the matter with the lights, Dani? Are they broken?" Sari asked.

"I don't know. Maybe a fuse blew. I'll have to wake up Papá."

Sari didn't speak, but the look on her face said it all. She would rather let sleeping Papás lie.

I knocked on the bedroom door and opened it a crack. "Papá? Papá, the lights aren't working. Can you check the circuit breaker?"

Papá rolled over and groaned. "I already checked," he said. "It's not the circuit. There must be a power cut in the whole building. Now leave me be."

I thought I remembered lights being on in the stairwell when we came home from school, but I apologized for waking him and shut the door.

"Sari, Papá says it's a power cut in the building. We'll just have to light a candle and pretend it's Shabbat. But first I'm going to run downstairs and get the mail before it gets too dark in the hallway."

"I don't want to stay here by myself," Sari whined.

"You're not by yourself. Papá is here."

Sari gave me a look that was way too old for her years. A look that said, *Yes, and he might as well not be.*

"All right, come with me. Let's go quickly, while there's enough light."

The strange thing was, as soon as I opened the apartment door, Sarita cried, "Dani, look, the lights are working!" because the hallway was lit. I tried the switch inside the apartment — still nothing. I puzzled over this as we walked downstairs to get the mail and then puzzled some more as we walked back up to the apartment carrying the daily collection of bills.

There was only one explanation I could think of, and I was carrying the answer in my hand. Cut-off notices. Had it come to that? Had we become so poor we couldn't even pay for basic necessities like lights? That could only mean one thing — that soon we'd lose our apartment, and the next stop would be living in cardboard boxes beneath an underpass.

"What is it, Dani? Why do you look so strange?"

I struggled to pull myself together for my little sister's sake.

"Oh, I'm just worrying about my algebra problems. Just wait till you have to do algebra."

"I'm really good with numbers," Sari said. "I'm one of the best in my class. Maybe I can help you."

I hugged her and kissed the top of her head. "Maybe. But first, let's have a cup of tea to keep us going."

As I headed to the stove to put the kettle on, I prayed that the gas hadn't been cut off, too.

There was more fighting after we'd gone to bed — but this time Mamá was really shouting.

"Eduardo, how long can this go on? Today, no electricity. Tomorrow, no gas. Next thing we can't afford the rent, and then we're out on the streets. Is that what you want for us? We have an opportunity to get out — we must take it!"

"But, Estela . . ."

"No buts, Eduardo. I've watched my children go hungry for long enough. I won't see them homeless, too. I'm going to call Jacobo collect tonight, like he says in the letter, and tell him to make the arrangements for us to come to America. Stay here if you like, Eduardo, but I'm taking the girls somewhere where we have an opportunity for a better life."

I let out a gasp from my eavesdropping spot behind the bedroom door. I couldn't believe my mother actually threatened to go without Papá. I couldn't believe that we were actually going to leave Argentina, where I'd lived my whole life. That we were going to America. I didn't know whether to feel relieved or frightened.

"You would leave me?" Papá said, sounding angry but also completely taken aback, like he couldn't believe what his ears had just heard. "Are you actually threatening to leave me, Estela, after . . . after all these years . . . after two children . . . after . . . everything we've been through together?"

I heard him take a deep breath.

"Are you asking me for a divorce?"

His voice shook slightly as he asked the question, and I realized he was scared, deathly scared, that Mamá might say yes. I was holding my breath, too, waiting to hear her answer.

"Eduardo, *el amor de mi vida*, of course I don't want a divorce," Mamá said, a tremor in her voice. "I want us to go to America *together*, the two of us and our girls, together as a family, so things will be better for us. I'm just desperate. Things can't go on the way they are now. I've been thinking about this, over and over, and this is the only way out. The situation here deteriorates every day. Look at us, sitting here in the twenty-first century with no electricity. If we're going to be doing things by candlelight, I want it to be because we're having a romantic evening, not because we can't afford the electric bill. Can't you understand that, *mi amor*?"

"I don't know what has come over you, Estela," Papá said, his voice icy. "You've changed. It's like I don't even know you anymore. My Stella wouldn't make threats like this."

"Maybe your Stella hadn't reached the point of desperation. Maybe your Stella is tired of seeing her husband behaving like he's given up."

"How dare you!" Papá shouted.

"Don't even think about raising a hand to me, Eduardo, or it *will* be divorce," Mamá said.

I jumped up, ready to go out and protect Mamá, but Papá said, "I'm going for a walk," and stormed out of the apartment, slamming the door behind him.

I heard Mamá weeping softly in the living room as I tried to go to sleep.

Papá was still asleep when I left for school the next morning. I didn't know what time he'd returned, but Mamá had deep circles under her eyes, as if she'd stayed awake all night waiting for him.

"Dani, you'll have to pick up Sarita today, because my shift doesn't end until seven," Mamá said. "And can you stop at the food bank at the synagogue and get some more food? We're running very low and I don't get paid till next week. Just don't say anything to your father."

No park with Roberto, I thought. But looking at the worry on Mamá's face, how could I possibly complain?

It was raining when I got out of school and I'd forgotten to bring an umbrella, so my uniform was wet and sticking to my skin by the time I got to Sarita's school to pick her up.

"*Hola*, Dani!" Sari called, skipping over to me. "Can we go to the playground on the way home? Please! Mamá's always too tired and I want to go on the swings."

"Not today, Sari."

"Pretty please?"

"No. We have to go to the synagogue, to the food bank."

She looked so disappointed that I felt bad. It wasn't like Sari had so many treats.

"Anyway, it's raining. You don't want to go on the swings in the rain, silly! How about I take you the next time the sun is shining?"

"You promise?"

"Tel lo juro," I said, kissing my index finger twice, which brought a smile back to Sari's face.

The rain had slowed to a drizzle by the time we reached the synagogue, but my heart sank because there was a long line outside the door. We weren't the only hungry Jews in Villa Crespo.

Sari was whining about being hungry and cold before we'd even waited ten minutes. I tried distracting her with tongue twisters: "Say '*Tres tristes tigres comen trigo en un trigal*' three times fast."

Sari's tongue got caught up on that one and she ended up in helpless giggles. I started her on *"Pepe pela papas pero pocas porque pisa pocas papas."* But I was starting to shiver myself. All I could think of were dry clothes and a hot cup of tea. I cursed myself for forgetting my umbrella, and hoped that Sari wouldn't get sick, because we wouldn't be able to afford the medicine to make her better.

By the time we got inside, Sari's teeth were chattering.

"You look cold, señorita. Would you like some hot chocolate?" one of the volunteers asked.

Sari nodded so hard her wet curls sent a spray of raindrops onto the floor.

"How about your big sister?" the volunteer asked, look-ing at me.

"*Sí, gracias.*"

While we waited for our food parcel, she brought us two Styrofoam cups of hot chocolate. It was only luke-warm, but it tasted so good that I almost cried from the pleasure of it.

"Your clothes are soaking wet," the volunteer said, clucking as she felt the sleeve of Sari's wet uniform blazer. "What size are you both? We just got a shipment of cloth-ing donations from abroad and there are some lovely things that might fit you. Let me take a look."

Sarita's eyes lit up at the prospect of new clothes, but I immediately thought of how we were supposed to explain them to Papá.

"Sari, even if she finds something, we can't wear it home," I warned her in a low voice.

"Why not?"

"You know why not."

Sari's lower lip stuck out, and I could see I was in for trouble. I couldn't argue, though, because another volun-teer returned with our food box.

"What's in there? Are there any cookies? Can I have something now?" Sari asked.

I looked through the box and found some crackers. Sari was munching on them when the first lady came back with a small bag of clothing.

"Here, take these. Why don't you go into the *servicio* and get changed so you don't catch cold?"

Sari was pulling clothes out of the bag and jumping up and down with excitement.

"Look, Dani! Look at this dress! It's so pretty! And this sweater! And look . . . some jeans for you. I'm going to get changed right now!"

I thanked the volunteer for her kindness, picked up the food box, and then dragged Sari over to the door.

"Sarita, I told you we can't go home dressed in new clothes. Papá will go crazy. You know how he is about taking charity. He's not supposed to even know we came here."

Sari stamped her foot. "I don't care about what Papá thinks. I'm cold and I want to wear my new clothes."

She glared up at me defiantly, and I was too tired and cold to fight her. Plus, I'd seen the pair of jeans in my size and it seemed like forever since I'd worn anything new, or even secondhand new.

"Okay. You win."

Sari threw her arms around my waist.

"I love you, Dani!"

We changed in the bathroom. Sari looked adorable in her new dress, and I felt wonderful in my new jeans and shirt. I had the rest of the walk home to figure out something to tell Papá.

*   *   *

"Be quiet when we get home," I warned Sari. "Maybe Papá will be sleeping."

We crept into the apartment, as quietly as we could. I hoped I could put the food away and get into our room to change before we encountered our father, but as Sari and I snuck into the kitchen, I heard "Daniela? Sarita? Is that you?"

"Yes, Papá," I called back.

I heard his footsteps coming from the living room, and quickly shoved the food box into the cupboard. But there was no way to hide our new clothes, or the bag containing our wet school uniforms.

He walked into the darkened kitchen and stopped, staring at Sarita in her dress.

"What is this?" he said, glaring at me. "Why aren't you in your school uniforms? And where did you get those clothes?"

"We got caught in the rain on the way home and I'd forgotten my umbrella," I said, giving Sari a "play along with me" look. "Our uniforms were soaked and I was worried about Sari catching cold, so I stopped at Sofia's place and borrowed some clothes. She has a sister Sari's age."

Sofia didn't have a little sister at all — she had an older brother. But I was hoping Papá wouldn't remember.

"Why didn't you just come straight home? I was worried because you were late," Papá said.

Of all the days for Papá to be awake and worrying instead of depressed and sleeping the afternoon away. Just my luck.

"I just thought . . . with the rain . . . and Sari . . . I didn't want her to get sick."

As if on cue, Sari sneezed loudly.

"Cover your mouth!" Papá chided. He gave me a long look. "Well, make sure you return the clothes to Sofia after Mamá washes them."

Thankfully, he turned his back to leave before he saw the look of horror on Sari's face.

"We don't have to give them back, do we?" she whispered.

"Don't worry, Sari. I'll think of a way for us to keep them."

I started to make dinner at seven, so that it would be ready by the time Mamá got home from work at seven thirty. But by eight o'clock she still wasn't home. We were sitting in the candlelight, getting more and more hungry, wondering where she was. Papá tried calling the hospital, to see if she'd been asked to stay late.

"I see. What? I'm sorry, our television isn't working, so . . ." His face paled. "¡Ay! I see. . . . Please call me right away if you hear anything. Gracias."

"Papá, what is it?" I asked, as soon as he'd hung up the phone.

"There's a big antigovernment demonstration going on near the hospital," he said. "Your mother might be caught up in it and . . . they say it's turned violent. People are breaking windows and looting stores. It's on the news, but we can't get the news because . . ." He punched the wall and shouted, *We don't have any goddamn electricity!*"

I felt sick, thinking of Mamá surrounded by an angry mob.

"I want Mami," Sarita cried. "When is she coming home?"

"Let's go read a story," I said. "Maybe by the time we're finished, Mamá will be home."

I read Sari a story by candlelight, and still Mamá wasn't back.

"When will Mamá be home?" Sari whined. "You said she'd be home after the story!"

"I said *maybe* she'd be home, not definitely. Look, why don't we have some dinner, and maybe while we're doing the dishes, Mamá will come through the door," I told Sari.

We sat picking at a dinner that, despite our hunger, none of us even wanted, waiting for the sound of Mamá's footsteps on the stairs. I told Sari to take the flashlight and go start running her bath while Papá called the hospital again. They still hadn't heard from Mamá.

"I'm going to go out and look for her," Papá said. "You stay here with Sarita."

"But what happens if you get lost, too?" I said, panicked.

"I can't just wait here, knowing she's out there with a riot going on, Dani," Papá said. "Something could have happened. She could be . . . hurt. I need to find her."

"But . . ."

Just then, we heard the sound of a key turning in the lock. We both rushed to the front door and there was Mamá. Her uniform was ripped and her face was bruised. She had a cut on her forehead and dried blood streaked her face.

"*D-os mío*, Estela!" Papá exclaimed, pulling her into his arms.

I hugged her, sandwiching her between Papá and me. I wanted just to touch her, to reassure myself that she was really there.

"Mamá, are you okay? What happened?"

"Let her sit down, Dani. And go make your *mamá* a cup of tea, with lots of sugar."

"*Mami!!!!!*" Sari came running to the door, and then saw the blood on Mamá's face and started crying. "Mami, what happened to you?"

She clung to Mamá's waist as if she would never let go.

Mamá stroked Sari's hair, and after detaching her from her waist, moved slowly toward the couch in the living room, as if each step pained her, with Sarita still gripping tightly to her hand. She sat down with a grimace and Sari cuddled up next to her.

"Dani, don't just stand there. I told you to make tea!" Papá said.

I'd been standing there, paralyzed: relieved that Mamá was home but terrified by the sight of her bruised, bloodied face. I headed into the kitchen and put the kettle on, and while I was waiting for it to boil, went to the bathroom for the first aid kit and some towels. I filled up a bowl with warm water and brought it to the living room, where Papá took the towels and gently started to wash the blood from Mamá's face.

When the tea was ready, I put in three heaping teaspoons of sugar, even though we hardly had any left, and brought it out to my mother.

"It was crazy, Eduardo," she was telling Papá. "I came out of the hospital and was waiting for the bus. . . . At first, it was just a peaceful demonstration, the usual *cacerolazo*, with pots and pans and shouting. I wasn't worried, just annoyed because the bus would be delayed. But then . . . out of nowhere things started to get violent. People were throwing rocks through store windows and looting . . . just taking things, Eduardo, like common criminals. . . . One of the rocks hit me in the head. . . . I fell. . . . People were stepping on me. . . ."

Sari was crying softly, "Mami . . . Mami . . . ," her face

buried in Mamá's lap. My father's face was grim. I felt sick to my stomach at the thought of my mother being trampled by a crowd of angry rioters.

"One man was kind enough to help me to my feet. I . . . should have gone back to the hospital but . . ." Mamá broke down, finally, and wept, her head bent over Sarita's dark curls. "I wanted . . . I needed . . . to be here . . . at home . . ." She looked up at Papá with tear-filled eyes. "With you."

Papá touched Mamá's cheek, gently, as if he were afraid she would break.

"Dani, take Sari and get her ready for bed," he said. "And you need to finish your homework. You both have school in the morning."

Sari didn't want to let go of Mamá, but Papá gave her a stern glance.

In the tub, the darkened bathroom lit only by a flashlight, Sari sat clutching her knees. "Why, Dani? Why would people hurt Mamá like that?"

"I don't think anyone *meant* to hurt Mamá. They were just desperate and angry and hungry and she happened to be in the wrong place at the wrong time."

Sari looked smaller than her seven years, naked and skinny in the bathtub, but when she raised her eyes to me they contained more anguish than a young child should ever suffer.

"I'm scared, Dani. Everything . . . everything is making me scared."

I held open a towel for her, and when she got out of the bath I wrapped her in my arms and hugged her for a long time.

"Me too, Sari. Me too."

Mamá had to read Sari two stories before she would go to sleep, and while she was doing that, I ran Mamá a hot bath so she could wash off the rest of the dirt and blood.

When Mamá was in her dressing gown, she sat with her arm around me on the sofa for a while, until it was time for me to go to sleep. The image of people stepping on her kept replaying itself in my mind, filling me with fear and anger.

"What will we do, Mamá?" I asked her.

I saw her glance over at Papá. He refused to meet her gaze.

"Don't worry, Dani," Mamá said. "Your father and I will make a decision for what is best."

Her voice was firm and decisive, despite everything she'd been through that evening, and I wondered if it meant that she'd decided to take us to America and leave Papá behind.

"Go to bed now, Dani. It's late, and Papá and I need to talk."

I kissed her, and said good night to my father. But I didn't get into bed. I sat behind the bedroom door and listened.

"So, Eduardo? Have you had a chance to think?"

There was silence, and I wished I could see the expressions on my parents' faces. Suddenly, I heard a strange, harsh sound coming from the living room.

"Eduardo, hush, everything is going to be okay," I heard Mamá's voice crooning softly.

Shocked, I realized it was the sound of my father sobbing.

"I can't lose you, Estela," Papá wept. "You're everything to me."

"Shhhhhh," Mamá said.

"When you were missing . . . when I thought something might have happened to you . . . it would have been the end of me, *querida*."

"I'm fine, Eduardo. Well, I've got a few cuts and bruises, but really, I'm all right."

"But you could have been seriously hurt." Papá let out a long, drawn-out sigh. "You win, Estela," he said, his voice soft and broken. "I can't fight you anymore. We will go to America."

"Oh, Eduardo!" Mamá said. It sounded like she'd started to cry again, but this time it wasn't from being sad. "This is the right thing. I know it."

"I'm frightened, *mi amor*. I'm forty-eight years old, no

longer a spring chicken. How am I supposed to start over again in a new country?"

"Because we'll do this together, *querido*. We'll give each other strength, just like we always have."

"How do we explain it to the girls?"

"We tell them the truth — that we're moving to America for opportunity, for hope, for a chance at a better life," Mamá said. "It's not like we're the first ones to leave. Dani told me the Sabans are moving to Miami, and the Tenenbaums made aliyah earlier this year."

"Well . . . what do you think about that, Estela? Are we better off moving to Israel?" Papá asked. "The Israeli government is offering great incentives. Maybe that would be better for us."

"But in America we have Jacobo," Mamá said. "Family is something, isn't it, if we're giving up everything else?"

"I've lost my sister, my parents, my business, and we're about to lose our apartment," Papá sighed. "Having family isn't just something; it's all we have left."

Chapter Four

*T*HE NEXT NIGHT over our candlelit dinner — we still had no electricity — my parents told us that we were moving to America. I acted surprised.

"America! So are we going to meet movie stars? And cowboys?" Sarita asked. "Oooh! Can we go to Disney World?"

"Don't be so stupid, Sari," I said. "We can't even afford to pay the electric bill; how do you expect us to go to Disney World?"

If looks could kill, I would have been buried in La Recoleta Cemetery with Evita Perón. I'm not sure whose glare was more deadly, Mamá's or Papá's. I felt bad when I saw Sari's lower lip start to quiver. What I said was the truth, but she was only seven. Why not let her dream a little?

"Someday we'll go to Disney World, *querida*," Mamá said. "But probably not right away."

"You promise, though? We'll definitely go someday?" Sari sniffed.

Mamá and Papá exchanged glances.

"We promise. Someday," Papá said gruffly.

Yeah, like when you're sixty, I wanted to say, but this time I was smart enough to keep my mouth shut.

"So when are we leaving?" I asked.

"As soon as we can get the visas and make the arrangements," Mamá said. "It takes longer since 9/11. I want you to work very hard on your English lessons in the meantime. The school year runs differently in America — not from March to December like here in Argentina. So if we get the visas in time, we'll leave when you have your winter break in July, then you'll start school at the beginning of their school year in September."

"So I won't even get a summer holiday?" I asked.

"No," Mamá said. "Because it will be winter in New York in December, not summer. The school year runs until the following June, and then you'll have a long vacation during the American summer."

Estupendo. Not only did I have to leave my country and start in a new school, but I had to live through a never-ending school year in order to do it. Still. It could have been worse. We could have stayed in Argentina and ended up living in a *villa mísera.* Given the alternative, going to school for a few extra months didn't seem like the end of the world. *Although*, said the cynical, pessimistic voice inside me, *that depends on the school, doesn't it?*

I told that voice to be quiet, because I had enough to worry about.

The following month was incredibly busy. We spent hours on line at the American Embassy, waiting to be interviewed for our visas. Sarita alternated between hyperactive excitement and whiny boredom, and I was always waiting for the moment when Papá would explode in front of all the other hopeful immigrants. Mamá and I took turns leaving the line to take Sari for walks, or to read to her from the English storybooks we took out of the library. We were all trying to practice our English as much as we could. Our conversations at home ended up being strange mixtures of Spanglish, where we'd start a sentence in English, then switch to Spanish when we didn't know the word. I was copying out words of vocabulary every night, trying to memorize at least forty new words a day. Roberto was doing the same, and we'd test each other as we walked to the park after school.

When our summer break started in mid-December and the date of his departure drew near, we spent even more time together, as much as we could. He met me outside my apartment one day with an "Adjectives for People" list that he'd gotten off the Internet.

"'Crazy,'" Roberto said.

"'*Loco*,'" I said. "Kind of how this is all starting to make me feel. Here's one . . . 'beautiful.'"

"'*Guapa*,'" Roberto said. "Like you, Dani."

I felt my cheeks flushing. "I'm sure you won't even miss me when you see all the 'beautiful' girls in Miami."

"Well, here's another word for you. They will all look 'ugly' to me, because they aren't you."

"'*Feo*,'" I said. "But I bet they won't. Still, it's nice of you to say."

I sighed, looking around the familiar streets, where we'd walked so many times before.

"Even though I know leaving Argentina is the right thing, I'm still 'sad' that we have to do it."

"'*Triste*,'" Roberto said. "Me too. 'Sad' to leave Argentina. 'Sad' to leave my home and my friends. 'Sad' to leave you, Dani."

He took my hand and gave it a gentle squeeze. "Still, *mi amor*. It's not going to be all bad, is it? Maybe we should try to think of the parts that are going to be 'interesting.' And 'exciting.'"

"'*Interesante y emocionante*,'" I said. "I know. There's a part of me that is excited to see what the future holds. Like do you ever wonder if life in America will really be like it looks on the TV shows?"

Roberto laughed. "I'm pretty sure the people in your

high school won't be as perfect looking. And if I'm wrong, I want to know about it right away so I can tell my parents to move to New York!"

His family was leaving the next day. Our remaining time together was so short and precious: so many memories to try to cram into a brief space. We reached our bench and I sat with my head on his shoulder, relishing the feel of his arm around me, the sensation of his lips brushing against my hair and my forehead. A nagging voice inside said I should be at home, helping Papá to look after Sarita while my mother was at work. I ignored the voice because I wanted this time with Roberto, I *needed* it, because for all I knew I would never have moments like this again.

The branches of the ombú tree reached over us like a mother's arms, as if to hug us to our native soil.

"Do you think we'll ever belong again, the way we do here?" I asked, between kisses. "Or do you think in America, we'll always be *extranjeros*? I mean, don't you hate what they call you on the visa — an 'alien,' like you come from outer space or something?"

Roberto attempted to soothe me with more kisses. He took his fingers and tried to smooth away the furrows in my brow.

"Dani, you worry too much."

"Yes, well, I think it's an inherited trait."

He laughed. "Well, try to relax. Do yoga. Meditate. Kiss me."

"I would kiss you with pleasure. Problem is, you aren't going to be around, are you?"

"True. And I don't want you kissing anyone else. So it'll have to be yoga or meditation." His lips met mine gently, and he brushed a loose strand of hair off my face. "Just try not to worry so much, *querida*. We'll adjust."

I threw my arms around his neck and burst into sobs. I couldn't believe that I wouldn't see him anymore, wouldn't feel his arms around me, or his lips on mine.

"Oh, Roberto . . . what will I do without you?"

"You'll survive, Dani. The same way I'll have to learn to live without you."

Roberto walked me back to my apartment. I must have looked like a vampire; my eyes were so red from crying.

"Well, I guess this is it, Dani," he said when we reached the corner where we always said our good-byes. My sight blurred with tears once more.

"You will . . . write me . . . won't you?"

He lifted my chin, so I was looking at him instead of the cracks in the sidewalk, where I'd focused to hide my tears.

"You think I'm going to walk away right now and you'll never hear from me again? Hah! You should be so lucky, Daniela Bensimon. . . . You can't get rid of Roberto Saban *that* easily."

I let out a really unattractive snort of laughter through

my tears, but that didn't seem to bother Beto. He wiped my tears away with his thumbs and kissed me again, for once not caring if my father happened to see.

"Just to make sure you don't forget me, I got you this," he said, taking a small box out of his pocket.

I opened it, and there on a thin silver chain was a small heart pendant.

"I had to fight with my father to let me have some of my Bar Mitzvah money to buy it," he said. "Not that my Bar Mitzvah money is worth a fraction of what it used to be."

He took it out of the box and helped me fasten it around my neck.

"Thank you, *querido*," I said. "I wish I could have bought you something."

"Don't worry," he said. "I have the pictures."

The week before, Beto had dragged me into one of those instant photo booths and we'd taken our picture together. The machine took four photos and he ripped the strip in half so we each had two.

"*Hasta la vista, mi amor*," Roberto said, and walked away down the street, looking back over his shoulder and blowing me one last kiss before he turned the corner out of sight.

I stood on the street, watching the empty space where I'd last seen him, feeling like my heart was breaking. Then I wiped my tears on my sleeve and headed home to rescue Sarita from Papá.

Chapter Five

IT WAS JULY 18, 2003, at nine fifty-three in the morning. It was also my birthday, the last one I would have in Argentina, so there wasn't much reason for joy. Nine years ago that day, a bomb ripped through the AMIA building, killing Tía Sara and all of the others. We were standing at 633 Pasteur Street in front of the black wooden panels with the names of the victims spray painted in white, and the photographs. I always found it so hard to look at them. When I saw Tía Sara's picture, smiling, happy, her dark curls, so like Sarita's, flowing over her shoulders, I expected her to walk out of the frame and embrace me. But she was trapped in the frame, her forever-smiling face inconsistent with the horrific way that she died.

When Tía Sara's name was called, we went up as a family. Papá lit a *yahrtzeit* candle and Mamá placed a red rose in a vase next to Tía Sara's picture.

As I watched the candles burning in front of the Wall of Memory, I wondered who would come now. When we were living five thousand miles away in America, who would be there to light a candle for Tía Sara, to honor her memory and say prayers for her soul in the place where she died?

Her parents were dead — her father, my *abuelo* Oscar, died of a heart attack six months after the bombing; the doctors said it was brought on by the stress. And my *abuela* Debora died last year, not long after Papá lost the business, of breast cancer. Sometimes I wondered if *that* had been brought on by the stress, too. With Tío Jacobo already in America, there would be no one left here to say kaddish, the memorial prayer for the dead. More than anything, that was what brought home to me the fact that we were going, that we were leaving Argentina for good.

My tears were for more than the bombing. For more than Tía Sara and the rest of the victims. I was crying for the future July 18s when we would be far away; where people might not understand why July 18 had such a dreadful meaning for us. I was crying for the following year, and the years after that, when Tía Sara's picture wouldn't have anyone to light a candle or place a rose. I was crying because I was scared of staying in Argentina, but I was scared of leaving, too. I was crying so hard that I set off Sarita.

Mamá's own eyes were wet, but she drew tissues from her bag and tried to calm the two of us.

"Come, girls, no more tears. Sari, you never knew your *tía* Sara, but Dani, you know how much she enjoyed life, how she looked forward to each and every day. Let's honor her memory by being happy, not by crying."

Easy for you to say. But I see the tears in your eyes, too.

Papá was acting completely shell-shocked. He'd become more and more remote as the date of our departure approached, and for him, being down on Pasteur Street always brought back memories of that awful day and night, the waiting, the interminable waiting without knowing if Tía Sara was alive. He walked as if he were moving through thick molasses, every step slow and sticky. I could see he wouldn't be much help with the final packing. It would all be down to Mamá and me, as so much had been in the last few months.

After the ceremony at Pasteur Street, we took the bus to the Jewish cemetery and visited Tía Sara's grave. We each found a smooth stone to place on the grave, instead of flowers, according to Jewish custom. Papá mumbled Mourner's Kaddish, and we stood looking at Tía Sara's headstone for what might be the last time. Who knew if or when we would be back to place another stone?

I went to find stones to place on my *abuelo* and *abuela*'s grave, too. I wanted them to know that they were remembered and loved, even if we would be far away in another land. It was so hard to leave Argentina when we were literally leaving our flesh and blood behind us.

"Are we doing the right thing, Abuela?" I whispered to my grandparents' headstone. "Will Papá be himself again, Abuelo? Do you think everything will turn out okay?"

The gravestone remained silent. All I could hear was the wind in the trees and the beating of my heart.

The night before, as a birthday present, Mamá had given me a little money so I could go have a cappuccino in one of the cafés on Avenida Corrientes with my remaining school friends, to celebrate my birthday and say good-bye. Roberto had sent me a birthday card with a picture of him leaning against a palm tree, wearing a Miami Dolphins T-shirt. David propped the picture up on the table with the salt and pepper shakers, so we could pretend that Beto was there with us.

My friends chipped in and bought some *alfajores* for us to share, and for that hour or so it almost felt like old times, before the Crisis, when we used to be able to do things like that all the time. So much so that sitting there with Sofia and Mili, Leo and David, I wondered if we were doing the right thing by leaving.

But as I walked home from the café in the chilly winter rain, past empty storefronts where there had been thriving businesses before the Crisis, I knew that the hour I'd spent with my friends, while fun, had been like an illusion: an escape from reality, not how things really were. Their families were suffering, too. It had been a big extravagance for all of us just to be in a café buying a coffee and some cookies, something two years ago we wouldn't have thought about twice.

Mamá must have scrimped and saved, because she found extra money to get chocolate to make a cake to eat on my actual birthday, July 18, Tía Sara's day, the night before we were leaving. It was supposed to be a surprise, but Sarita was so excited about it she let it slip.

"Dani, I can't wait for after dinner because we're having a cake for you and it's your favorite, chocolate!" she told me. "But don't tell anyone because it's a surprise."

I struggled to keep a straight face, but promised to keep it a secret.

I think I acted surprised enough to fool Mamá when she brought out the cake. Sari was jumping around the kitchen table, so hyper that I was afraid Papá would start shouting at her, but he was still in the far-off place where he'd retreated down at Pasteur Street.

Even though I'd been dreaming about it for months, I'd forgotten just how good chocolate cake tasted. Sari, Mamá, and I each had two pieces. Papá had one, but I wondered if he even tasted it.

He went to bed right after dinner, despite the fact that

there was all the last-minute packing to do. I wished I could tune out the world the way he did. Sarita was the total opposite. She was so excited about going on her first airplane, an excitement only heightened after the chocolate cake, that I was worried she'd be up all night.

"So how does the plane get off the ground if it's filled with all the people and the luggage and everything? Isn't it too heavy?"

"No, Sari. It has very big engines to help it lift off, and then there are laws of thermo-something-or-other. Thermodynamics, I think it's called. You'll learn about it when you're older."

"But you're older and you don't know about it."

"That's because I haven't taken physics yet."

"What do you think it's like in America? Do you think I'll make friends?"

Sari might have been eight years younger than me, but we were still worrying about the same things.

"I'm sure you'll make friends," I assured her. "After all, who wouldn't want to be friends with someone as wonderful as you?"

Sarita smiled and threw her arms around me.

I only wished I could say the same thing to myself and believe it.

She finally snuggled into bed with her scrap of blanket, her Baba, but just as I thought she was about to drift off she sat up and asked, "We'll be able to take Baba with us to America, won't we?"

I went over and stroked her forehead. "Of course, Sari. Baba can come with us on the plane. We'll pack it in your hand luggage tomorrow morning, first thing, before we leave for the airport."

"You promise?" she said. "You won't forget?"

"I won't forget. I promise."

But just in case, I searched around for a piece of scrap paper and a pen and wrote BABA in big letters, then placed it on the floor by my bed where I'd be sure to see it.

Mamá and I lay on the floor in the empty living room, after Sarita had gone to sleep and we'd finished packing the last suitcase.

"*Ay*, my back," Mamá sighed. "I'm not looking forward to heaving those suitcases through the airport tomorrow."

"Well, Papá should carry them. It's the least he can do since we did all the work."

"Dani, that's enough. Don't speak to me about your father in that tone of voice. It's been a hard enough day without having to listen to you snipe at Papá."

It drove me crazy how Mamá defended Papá all the time, how she expected me to respect him when he'd done nothing to make himself deserving of my respect. We had been doing most of the work, she and I. Papá just . . . went to sleep. Why couldn't she acknowledge that?

"I can't believe it's here already. That we're leaving tomorrow," Mamá said. "It's been like a whirlwind, getting everything ready in such a short time, that I haven't had much time to think. But today . . . today at Pasteur Street, it really hit me that we are going — that we won't be there next month or next year or the year after."

So Mamá had felt it, too.

She grasped my hand. "This is hard, Dani. So very hard. But I know in my heart that we're doing the right thing by leaving."

"How do you know, Mamá? How can you be so sure?"

"Faith, Dani. I have faith."

I wish I shared it.

"Trust me, *querida*. Things are going to be better for us in America. I'm sure of it."

"Well, I guess I better try to get some sleep," I said, dragging myself off the floor. "Do you want a hand getting up?"

"No," Mamá said. "Your father is probably snoring. I think I'm just going to lie here for a while."

I lay awake for hours, listening to Sarita's even breathing and the faint but familiar noises from the street below.

It was hard to imagine that the following evening I'd be sleeping in a strange bed in another country. I wasn't sure if it was nerves or the chocolate cake, but my stomach was churning. When I finally did manage to fall asleep, my dreams were filled with bombed buildings and *yahrtzeit* candles, with airplanes and American flags and Roberto and the ombú tree.

Chapter Six

$\mathcal{T}$HE LAST DAY. The last morning in my own bed. Mamá's brother, my *tío* Arturo, had woken up at dawn to travel from Córdoba so he could drive us to the airport and then help dispose of what little furniture we had left after we'd gone. My feet felt heavy against the floor as I got out of bed, my heart equally heavy in my chest as I brushed my teeth and hair. It was the last time I'd see my reflection in the mirror that I'd watched myself grow up in; it was the last time I'd spit in that sink. Every little thing seemed to take on a disproportionate importance because it was the last time I'd do it in the place I'd always known. From that day on, everything was going to be different. A different apartment, a different school, a new circle of friends (hopefully), a different language, a different country. All change.

I wondered if this was how a snake felt right before it shed its skin and slithered along without everything that identified it before. Does a snake worry about missing that skin? Or does the snake not even notice as it just keeps moving forward?

Mamá shouted for me to hurry up in the bathroom, so we weren't late for the airport. I took one final glance at myself in the old familiar mirror, fingering the heart necklace that Beto had given me, and whispered, *"Adiós, amiga."*

Then I hurried back to my room to get dressed and finish packing. I slid the photo booth portraits of Beto and me and all of his and Gaby's letters into my suitcase. Then I saw the sign I'd made the night before, and made sure that Baba was packed in Sari's backpack.

I'd never been to Ezeiza International Airport before. It was thirty-five kilometers out of the city. I sat staring out of the window, my feet on top of my hand luggage in Tío Arturo's packed car as it wound its way through the traffic, out of Villa Crespo, away from the familiar streets.

We passed landmarks I'd known all my life, and I wondered if I would ever see them again, if this was a permanent good-bye, or if some day we would return to Buenos Aires, even if just for a visit.

Sarita was excited and chattering nonstop, squeezed in the backseat between Mamá and me.

"Can I sit next to the window in the plane since you got to sit next to the window in the car?" she asked, squirming and leaning over me for a better view. "That's fair, right?

What do you think it'll be like in America? Is the weather warmer or colder than it is here?"

Papá finally told her to hush because she was giving him a headache, and she leaned her head against my shoulder. When I dragged my eyes away from the window to look at her, I noticed a tear running down her cheek.

I brushed it away gently with my knuckles and wondered again if things would be different for us when we got to America. Would being on a new continent magically transform my father back into the Papá of Before? Would he stop moping around the apartment; would he find the energy to be someone again? Someone laughing, kind, and gentle, instead of the unpredictable, angry, bitter man he had become?

As much as I hated to leave Argentina, as much as I was afraid of what lay ahead of us, it would be worth all the changes, I thought, all the upheaval we were going through, if we got our old Papá back.

It took a long time to check in at the airport, and Papá was getting more irritable by the minute.

We had to part with Tío Arturo before we went through security. I could tell Mamá was trying hard to be brave in front of Sarita and me, but when she faced her brother and finally had to say good-bye, she fell into his arms and wept. Tío Arturo had tears in his eyes, too.

"Estela, *hermana*, take good care of yourself and my

beautiful nieces. Make sure you write to me often. Maybe I'll even get Tomás to take me to the Internet café to show me how to use the computer so we can e-mail."

"You think he can teach an old dog like you new tricks?" Mamá joked through her tears, stroking Tío Arturo's cheek tenderly.

"Well, if I'm old, little sister, you aren't too far behind."

Tío Arturo turned to me and hugged me tightly.

"Be a good help to your *mamá*, Dani," he whispered in my ear. "She'll need all the help you can give her."

"I know," I whispered back.

"You're a good girl, Dani. We'll miss you, your *tía* Sophia and me, and your cousins Tomás and Mateo."

"We'll miss you, too, Tío Arturo," I said, feeling my own tears starting to well up.

"We should go," Papá said. I think he wanted to get us moving before Mamá broke down crying again.

Tío Arturo said good-bye to Sari and hugged Mamá one last time. Then we walked into the restricted zone, waving until the doors closed and we couldn't see him anymore.

After we went through security I offered to take Sarita to see the shops, to give Mamá a chance to recover and to get Sari away from Papá for a while.

We tried on sunglasses and tested perfume in the duty-free, until the smell started to make Sarita feel sick. That's all I needed, to have my sister puke on me on the plane, when I didn't have anything else to change into. That would definitely not be the way to start my life in a new country — reeking of younger-sibling vomit.

I dragged Sari out of the duty-free to get some fresh air. Worried that Papá might make some comment about how we smelled like women of ill repute, I searched out a ladies' room to try and wash off some of the perfume smell.

We were washing our wrists at the sink when an American family came in, talking loudly. I was trying hard to follow their conversation, but they were speaking very quickly, and it suddenly struck me that soon all the conversations I was going to have to follow would be in English, that I was always going to be having to think about what was being said as I was doing right then, instead of just automatically understanding it, like I would in Spanish.

It made my brain hurt.

"Come, Sari, let's get back to Mamá and Papá. We don't want to miss our flight."

As I walked back down the concourse with Sari, I kept thinking, *This is the last time I'll be here, this is my last hour in Argentina, I might never be in my country again.*

I wondered if Gaby and Roberto felt this way when they left.

I tried to sleep on the ten-hour flight, but between Sarita squirming next to me and the snoring man in front of me who put his seat back so far his head was practically in my lap, it felt as if I'd only just closed my eyes before the lights came on and the flight attendants were telling us to place our seats in the upright position for our descent into New York. My eyes were gritty from the dry air and lack of sleep. I felt like I was in a waking dream, that at any moment I might blink and be back in Buenos Aires. Except that everything about my old life was gone, and like the snake without its skin, I just had to keep moving forward.

Papá had to carry Sarita off the plane because she was so sleepy, so of course I ended up having to carry his hand luggage, as well as my own, like a human packhorse. Tío Jacobo was supposed to be meeting us when we got through customs, to drive us to the suburban town of Twin Lakes, New York, where we'd be living.

As we waited in the interminable line to show the man our passports, I tried to imagine what Twin Lakes would look like. Even though I knew that New York was nothing like the Swiss Alps, there was something about the name, Twin Lakes, that made me picture a cool Alpine lake surrounded by mountains that were reflected in its crystalline surface.

I sensed Mamá's tension as the line moved us closer to the Passport Man. Ever since the Dirty War, Mamá had an almost irrational fear of people in uniform, because of what happened to her cousin Enrique, the one who was "Disappeared."

"Stay close to me and don't say anything," Mamá whispered as we shuffled up to the yellow line. Beads of sweat gathered on her forehead.

"Step forward, please," called the official from behind his desk.

Of course, Sarita picked that moment to wake up. She lifted her head from Papá's shoulder and looked straight at the official.

"*¿Donde estamos? ¿Estamos en los Estados Unidos?*"

"*Sí,*" the man said in American-accented Spanish. "You're in America now, young lady."

He asked us how long we were staying. Papá showed him the visa stamped from the embassy in Buenos Aires, all the papers arranged with Tío Jacobo. Mamá gripped my hand, her face pale. I was afraid she was going to faint or have a heart attack. But finally the man took out his rubber stamp and marked each of our passports with a loud *thump* before handing them back to Papá.

"*Ay*, I thought he was going to send us back to Buenos Aires," Mamá whispered as we walked toward the baggage claim in search of a luggage cart.

"Everything's going to be okay, Mamá," I told her. "We're in America now."

I just wished I could convince myself of that.

The baggage area was crowded and noisy with crying children and people complaining about their lost suitcases.

As we waited for the luggage from our flight to arrive, I silently prayed that my bag wasn't lost. We were allowed to bring so little with us from home, just one suitcase from an entire lifetime. If that was lost, then I really was starting from nothing, without my photos of Roberto and my letters from him and Gaby. I clutched my heart necklace tightly. At least I had that. I never took it off, ever, not even when I slept.

Thankfully, all our luggage showed up, although we had to wait quite a while for Sarita's suitcase, and she was getting very whiny — and Papá very irritable — by the time it came down the conveyor belt.

When we finally emerged through the sliding doors of the arrivals hall, there was a crowd of people waiting. People all around us were giving cries of joy and welcome, greeting their loved ones with hugs and flowers and balloons and teddy bears. I glanced over at Papá for guidance, but he looked just as confused and frightened as I felt.

"*¿Dónde está Jacobo?*" Mamá muttered, pushing through the crowd with the luggage cart. "Dani, hold tight to Sarita. I don't want her to get lost in this madhouse."

There wasn't much chance of that. Sari was clutching my hand tightly; I could barely feel my fingertips. Her eyes were opened so wide I could see the whites around her irises as she took in the unfamiliar scene around her. I knew how she was feeling. Everything was so different —

the sights, the sounds, and the smells. I kept my eyes firmly fixed on the familiar pattern on the back of my mother's flowered shirt.

"Eduardo! *¡Bienvenido!* Welcome!"

My *tío* Jacobo was weaving his way through the crowd, holding a bunch of flowers and two small flags on sticks, one Argentinean and one American. He threw his arms around Papá, and when they released each other, their eyes were wet with tears.

He handed Mamá the flowers, then held his arms open to give her a hug.

"Estela, *querida, bienvenida a los Estados Unidos*! Welcome to America."

And then it was my turn to be enveloped in his embrace, along with Sarita, since she still wouldn't let go of my hand.

"Daniela. Sarita. *¡Que bellas sobrinas!* I'm so glad you are here in America now, so we can see each other more often. I've missed seeing you grow up."

He noticed Sarita eyeing the flags. "And these are for you, *cosita linda*, now that you are going to be a proper Argentinean American!"

Sarita smiled shyly and took the flags, finally releasing her death grip on my hand to do so. She waved them to and fro; people around us smiled and one woman said, "Look at that little girl, isn't she adorable?"

Sarita had that effect on people.

"Come, you must be exhausted," said Tío Jacobo. "This way to the car."

He picked up Sarita and led the way through the crowd and out of the building. The heat and steamy humidity hit like a wall the minute we left the air-conditioned terminal. It was hard to believe that it was winter when we left Argentina, and we'd worn our jackets on the way to the airport.

"Here, let me push that for you," I said to Mamá, who had sweat running down her face as she struggled with her cart.

"*Gracias, querida,*" Mamá said, breathing heavily as she handed the cart over to me.

"Are you all right?" I didn't want Mamá to have a heart attack. I couldn't imagine how we would all survive if anything happened to her.

"Yes, I'm fine. It's just so hot."

She took a tissue from her bag and wiped the sweat from her face. "And the humidity — *ay!*"

We crossed a busy street of taxis and buses and cars. People were honking their horns and a policeman kept blowing his whistle and yelling at drivers to keep moving. It's not like the airport in Buenos Aires wasn't noisy and full of hustle and bustle, but this was a strange and different hustle and bustle. Everything was strange and different. Or maybe it was just *me* that was strange and different.

I kept my eyes on the back of Tío Jacobo's head and Sarita's waving flags, and finally we got to an old sedan car with Argentinean and American flag stickers on the back bumper, and a bumper sticker with the outline of the Twin Towers and "9/11 Never Forget." As if anyone ever could.

"Here we are," Tío Jacobo said, lowering Sarita to the ground and getting out his keys.

It took ten minutes of pushing and shoving and muttered swearwords with Mamá covering Sarita's ears before all the luggage would fit into the car. I ended up with a suitcase on my lap and hand luggage under my feet, which made it hard to see anything out of the front of the car, but at least I could look out of the side window.

At first all I could see were houses and the highway. But then Tío Jacobo pointed out Shea Stadium. "That's where the Mets, one of New York's baseball teams, play." There was a huge sculpture of a globe in a park in front of the stadium, and Tío Jacobo said that it was called the *Unisphere* and was put there for a World's Fair that was held in 1964.

Sarita's head lolled against my shoulder. As excited as she was, she couldn't keep her eyes open after the long flight. My eyelids felt heavy, but my nerves were taut with excitement.

Then, as we approached a bridge, the Whitestone Bridge, Tío Jacobo told us to look to the left as we crossed. And there it was — the New York City skyline. Just as Beto and I pictured it as we walked through the leafy streets of Buenos Aires and imagined ourselves somewhere else. I wondered where Roberto was and what he was doing right at that moment, down in Miami. His letters spoke of wide white beaches and palm trees, of buildings painted in pastel shades of blue and pink and yellow. New York seemed washed of all color by a haze of humidity that hung over the city like a translucent cloak. Still, at least we were in the same country, in the same time zone even.

"Look, Mamá, you can see the Empire State Building!" I exclaimed.

"And the tall building with the triangular top, that's the Citigroup building," Tío Jacobo said. "After it was built, the structural engineer realized there was a design problem and some of the bolted joints might not stand up to winds over seventy miles per hour."

"*¡D-os mío!*" Mamá exclaimed. "What did they do?"

"Well, without telling the public about the danger, the owners had thick steel plates welded over the joints," Tío Jacobo said. "They had it done at night, after the office workers had gone home for the day. They managed to keep it a secret for almost twenty years, believe it or not."

"Sounds like something that would happen in Argentina," Papá grumbled.

I made a mental note to never go up to the top of the Citigroup building, especially if it was windy.

It was like watching a movie, seeing the skyline as we

drove across the bridge. But then, nothing seemed real. I kept thinking that the following morning I'd wake up back in our apartment in Buenos Aires, that I'd go back to school at the Escuela Hebrea with Señor Guzmán and Gaby and Beto. But I had to remind myself that that was no longer my reality; from that moment on, I was going to have to find myself a new one.

After the bridge, there was more highway, and my eyelids drifted shut. The next thing I knew, Mamá was shaking me awake.

"Come, Dani. We're here! Help with the luggage!"

We were in front of a small, nondescript-looking red-brick building on a quiet, leafy street. "Welcome to Twin Lakes, New York," Tío Jacobo said. "I called Mrs. Ehrenkranz, from Jewish Family Services, and she should be here any minute with the key to the apartment."

I looked around. It was nothing like the Alpine village of my imagination. There were no mountains, no cool, crystalline lake. Heat shimmered off the sidewalk in the sunny patches between the shade of the trees.

We'd unloaded most of the bags when a car pulled up and a well-dressed woman emerged.

"*¡Buenos días!* I'm Jane Ehrenkranz, from Jewish Family Services. Welcome to the United States, and to Twin Lakes," she said, shaking hands with Papá and Mamá. "You must be exhausted from your trip. Let's get you inside, so you can get settled."

We all carried suitcases — even Sarita took some of the hand luggage — up two flights of stairs. Mrs. Ehrenkranz stopped to open the door, and then we crowded into the hallway of what would be our new home in America.

It was hot and smelled of something unfamiliar.

"Let me get the air conditioner going," said Mrs. Ehrenkranz. "It hasn't been running while the apartment was empty."

She went to a box on the wall and started to fiddle with the controls. Tío Jacobo said, "Eduardo, why don't you come look at this to see how it works?"

Papá shuffled over, leaving Mamá and Sarita and me to survey our new surroundings. The living room was decorated, if you could call it that, with a large sofa that had seen better days, a large rectangular coffee table, and two end tables with mismatched lamps on them. The carpet was a nondescript beige that had clearly just been cleaned but was worn in places. At least the walls looked okay — the living room smelled of fresh paint.

We followed Mamá down the short, dark hallway. There was one medium-sized room with a double bed, and a smaller room with two twin beds. The compact bathroom contained a shower and a toilet. No bathtub.

Sarita said what I was thinking. "Mamá, I don't like this place. I want to go home."

"Quiet, Sari!" Mamá said. "It's a roof over our heads. It will do just fine."

"But . . . why can't we stay with Tío Jacobo?"

"Because he lives in a tiny studio apartment and there is no room for us. We're lucky that because of the Crisis in Argentina, Jewish organizations are willing to provide help to immigrants like us."

"But, Mamá," Sari whined. "It's . . ."

"Shush!"

Sarita's eyes filled with tears and I put my arm around her shoulders.

"I know how you feel," I whispered into her dark curls. "I'm not exactly in love with this place, either."

She buried her face in my side.

"Come on, let's go choose which will be your bed," I said.

Mamá looked back at me gratefully, on her way to go investigate the tiny kitchen.

Sarita chose the bed closest to the window. Not that it really mattered. There were only about six inches between the two beds. It was going to be a tight squeeze. So much for having any privacy.

Tío Jacobo stuck his head in the room.

"I'm leaving now. I have to get to work. Mrs. Ehrenkranz will stay for a while to help you get settled in. Tomorrow we will get you registered for school."

He came over to give us each a kiss and a hug. "I'm so happy to have my nieces living nearby. I've missed you so."

We followed him out to the living room, where Mamá and Papá were sitting on the sofa talking to Mrs. Ehrenkranz. Mamá looked worried and Papá . . .

"What do you mean, counseling?" he exploded. "How dare you suggest that we need counseling, like we're *locos*, just because we've come from Argentina!"

"Mr. Bensimon, I wouldn't dream of suggesting . . . It's nothing to do with that, it's merely a suggestion because sometimes when people have made such a big transition, especially after having been through a difficult situation like you have —"

"Get out! Get out of here. Let us unpack our bags in peace with some dignity, without you insulting us!"

"Eduardo," Mamá pleaded, "*basta*, enough. She didn't mean anything by it. . . ."

"Out!"

"Eduardo, *basta*!" Tío Jacobo said sternly. "Stop this."

But Papá wouldn't be stopped. He continued to rant, telling Mrs. Ehrenkranz to leave. Sarita was clinging to me, hiding her face in my T-shirt. I wanted to sink into the floor when I saw the look on Mrs. Ehrenkranz's face — the combination of pity, fear, and shock.

Finally, Mamá ushered her out the door. Sarita and I followed them to get away from Papá.

"I'm sorry," Mamá said in a low voice. "When he gets like this . . ."

"Please don't apologize," Mrs. Ehrenkranz said. "I realize that you've been under a great deal of pressure and that you've just had the stress of a very big move." She handed Mamá a card. "Feel free to call me. *Anytime.*"

Tío Jacobo was talking to Papá in a low, angry voice when we got back into the living room.

"Girls, take your suitcases and go get unpacked," Mamá said.

As I put my meager supply of clothes into the scratched wooden dresser, and helped Sarita do the same, I heard Papá's and Tío Jacobo's raised voices through the thin walls.

We might have moved five thousand miles, but we were still living with the same angry man. We were just doing it in a smaller apartment, in a strange country where we didn't know anyone except Tío Jacobo. What fun.

Chapter Seven

Tío Jacobo picked us up the next morning to take us to register for school. We went to the elementary school first. It was much bigger than the day school in Buenos Aires, but the corridors were bright and cheerful, even in the summer with no artwork hanging on the walls. There was at least one computer in every classroom, and an entire room of them in a special lab off the well-stocked library, or "media center." But none of this impressed Sarita as much as the playground outside.

"Look, Dani!" she said, climbing up the side of a huge wooden boat, and then sliding down a circular slide. "Isn't this *estupendo*?"

The only thing that was *estupendo* about Twin Lakes High School, where I was to attend school, was its size. It was enormous. I couldn't imagine how I would ever manage to find my way around. You could fit most of my old school in Buenos Aires into the gymnasium.

"Too bad your school doesn't have a playground like my school," Sarita said, as we piled into Tío Jacobo's car.

"No, instead I just have a long list of books to read — in English!"

"Jacobo, can we stop at the library on the way home so Dani can get the books she needs?" Mamá asked. "She better get started right away if she's going to get through that list before school begins."

In some ways, it was a good thing I had no friends and no life, because it meant I had no distractions from my schoolwork. At least after our visit to Twin Lakes Memorial Library, I was the proud owner of my very own library card, which meant I could use the computers there free of charge if I wanted to go online. I couldn't wait to get back there so I could write a long e-mail to Roberto, or try to IM him even. I had a feeling I'd be spending a lot of time at the library.

When Tío Jacobo dropped us back at the apartment, Papá told us "that woman, Mrs. Ehrenkranz" had stopped by and left some bags of clothing for Sarita and me. We rushed into our room and sure enough, there were two large black garbage bags, one on each bed.

Sarita dumped hers out onto the floor and started dancing around in ecstasy. "Look, Dani! Look at this skirt! Look at this sweater!"

She put on the sweater and the skirt over the clothes she was wearing, and then picked up a pink dress with a ruffled hem and held it close to her body. "Look at this! Isn't it pretty?"

I opened my bag and started taking out clothes. There were jeans and shirts and skirts and dresses, some of them from designer labels that were recognizable even to me. Big names. Global names. Names I'd only ever dreamed of being able to wear on my rear end, especially since Papá lost the clothing store.

"Try them on!" shouted Sarita. "Let's do a fashion show for Mamá!"

I pulled out a bright green sundress, embroidered with little pink flamingos. The colors were so flamboyant, so unlike what I was used to wearing, that I couldn't picture myself in it. But I was in a new country, living a new life. Couldn't I create a new me to go with it? I could be an American girl, someone who would feel at home in a dress like that. A girl with friends. Lots of new American friends.

I pulled off my shorts and T-shirt and pulled the dress over my head.

"So, what do you think?"

Sari jumped up and down, clapping.

"Pretty! You look so pretty! Come, let's show Mamá!"

I hummed a song as we strutted down the hallway to the kitchen.

"Look, Mamá!" Sari cried.

She did a twirl for Mamá, and then sashayed into the living room to show off for Papá.

"Don't I look pretty, Papá?"

Papá scowled. "It's bad enough we have to take charity. You don't have to go around flaunting it."

Sari had been prancing around the living room on her tiptoes like a little sprite, but at my father's words it was as if someone turned off a light switch inside her. Her face crumpled, and she ran out into the hallway toward our bedroom.

At that moment, I felt a rush of hatred toward Papá, so powerful that it frightened me. My fists clenched as if to hit him. I knew Papá hated taking charity; seeing his children in hand-me-down clothes was especially painful for someone who used to own a clothing store and dress them in the latest fashions. But still.

"Eduardo," Mamá said. "Did you have to? She's just a child, for heaven's sake! Let her enjoy herself."

"What is there to enjoy? Living in this tiny apartment in a strange country, taking charity from strangers."

Mamá sighed. "Eduardo, please. *Querido*, I know it's hard for you, but we've talked about this. It's a new beginning, with new opportunities. You need to change your attitude."

"What opportunity? Who is going to hire a middle-aged Argentinean man who ran a family business? What am I going to do here? Tell me that, Estela! What am I going to do?"

It was hard to believe I'd actually felt optimistic when I

put on that stupid flamingo dress. I ran down the hall to join Sarita in our room.

She was lying on the bed, curled up in a ball. She'd taken off her cute new outfit, and shoved all the clothes back into the big black garbage bag.

I lay down on the bed next to her and curled myself around her, drawing comfort from the warmth of her body.

"W-will Mamá tell Mrs. Ehrenkranz to take the clothes back?" Sarita said, the tremor in her voice giving away the fact she was on the verge of tears.

I tucked one of her curls behind the pink shell of her ear.

"No, Sari, I'm sure she won't. Mamá is way too sensible for that. She knows we need new clothes, and these are much nicer than what we could afford to buy ourselves."

I tickled her, and she started to squirm.

"Besides, you looked way too adorable in that outfit to even *think* about giving it back."

One great thing about Sarita is that she doesn't sulk for long. The mention of her adorableness was like a magic wand. She leaped out of my arms and danced to the end of the bed to catch a glimpse of herself in the mirror perched on top of the chest of drawers.

We spent the next hour trying on the rest of the clothes, but we kept the fashion show to ourselves. And I ended up having to fold them all and put them away at the end of it.

But it was worth it, just to see the smile back on my little sister's face.

Mrs. Ehrenkranz found Mamá a job as a personal care assistant for a wealthy elderly couple in Twin Lakes. To get there, Mamá had to take a bus and then walk half a mile, but we couldn't afford to get a car yet. It also meant that once school started, I would have to come straight home, meet Sarita at her bus, make sure she did her homework, and make dinner, because Mamá didn't get home until after six o'clock.

There was a part of me that wanted to ask, *Where's Papá in all of this? Why can't he do any of the work?* But the words stayed stuck in my throat, even though it felt at times like they were choking me.

Mamá liked the couple she worked for, Mr. and Mrs. Binen. She said we wouldn't believe their house — marble sinks and floors in the bathrooms, closets as big as the bedroom I shared with Sarita, and a big outdoor swimming pool, even though both of them were too infirm to use it. They kept it open for their children and grandchildren when they came to visit, Mamá said.

"Can we go swimming there?" asked Sarita. "Please, Mamá?"

"No, Sari, we can't," I told her. "It's not like that. Mamá's kind of . . . you know, like a servant in their house."

I missed Mamá's warning glance, but it was impossible to miss Papá's fist smashing down on the kitchen table.

"Don't you *ever* call your mother a servant!" he shouted. "Bensimons are not *servants* to anyone!"

I bowed my head and mumbled, "Sorry, Mamá," then escaped to my room.

It was impossible to know what was allowable to say or do in our house, what would trigger the next explosion from Papá. I wished I could be the one to go out to work and let Mamá be home with Sarita. Why did I have to be the one stuck in the apartment with Papá?

In the few weeks before school started, Sari and I took walks around the neighborhood to get familiar with our surroundings. One day we rode the bus from one end of the route to the other, just to get out of the apartment and away from Papá. But our favorite place to go was the library, because we could walk there easily and it was air-conditioned. I would take Sari to the children's section and read her books, then let her choose a few to take home. Then I'd go to the public computers and send e-mails to Gaby and Beto. One day, I logged into MSN and Beto was online, too, so I actually got to chat with him.

Beto!

Hola Dani!

I've missed you sooooooooooooooooooo much!

Me too. Everyone OK?

It's been crazy. Mama's started her new job. Sari and I have been busy exploring.

Made friends yet?

No. Haven't met anyone. But school starts next week, so hopefully . . .

Yeah, you'll meet people there for sure. I start tomorrow. Can't believe summer is over already.

I'm still getting used to the fact that it IS summer. In August!

I know. Had to get used to that whole Northern Hemisphere thing.

I miss you.

I know. Me too.

"Can we go now?" Sarita whined. "I'm bored."

"In a minute. I'm chatting to Beto," I said.

"How? He's not here. And I don't hear you talking. Anyway, you're not supposed to talk in the library."

"No, silly, I'm chatting to him online. Just wait a minute, okay? Read your books."

Sorry, Beto, Sari here and getting restless. Using computer in the library.

My dad just got one at home, because he needs it for work. Hopefully he's going to pass medical boards soon and then he can get started working as a doctor again.

Lucky you! And that's great about your dad.

I didn't mention that my *papá* was still depressed and I hoped he wouldn't ask.

I still have all your letters, Beto.

Me too. But easier to e-mail now that you can go to the library.

I know. But I still love your letters ☺

☺

Sari pulled at my arm. "Dani, I'm hungry and I have to pee. Can't we go now?"

I sighed. "One more minute."

Sari started whispering: "One, two, three, four, five, six . . ."

I wanted to scream.

Beto, amor, I have to go. Sari is driving me crazy.

Okay. Well, talk to you soon. Muchos besos.

Besos xoxox

Somehow, even though Beto and I were in the same country, it didn't feel like it. He felt so far away at that moment he could have been on the moon.

Chapter Eight

$\mathcal{I}$ WOKE UP AT SIX on the first day of school, because I had to be at the bus stop at seven. It seemed inhumanly early, but I was so nervous about making a good first impression that even though I'd picked out what to wear the night before, I tried on another few choices just in case. I started to long for my old school uniform, something I never thought I'd do, ever.

In the end I went with the original outfit, a pair of jeans and an embroidered cotton shirt with French labels. Whoever donated the clothes to Jewish Family Services didn't just have good taste — they had lots of money.

Sarita was still curled up in bed, but Mamá was waiting for me in the kitchen.

"You have to eat breakfast, Dani," she said.

"I'm too nervous to eat anything. I feel sick."

She made me a cup of tea and two pieces of toast anyway, and stood over me until I forced them down.

"I know this is hard, *amorcita*, but you'll be fine," Mamá said. "Tío Jacobo says that Twin Lakes High is a very good school, despite being so big. I know you miss your friends, but you'll make new ones. You're so smart and beautiful."

She was fiddling with my hair.

"Okay, Mamá, *basta*. You're just making me more nervous."

I grabbed my book bag, which was filled with what seemed like a fortune's worth of new notebooks and pens, all required, according to the supplies list, and headed for the door.

"You have the lunch voucher?"

Sarita and I qualified for a subsidized school lunch program. I wished I could just take food from home or buy lunch with money like everyone else.

"Yes, Mamá," I sighed.

She planted a kiss on my forehead.

"Good luck, *querida*."

There were already three people waiting at the bus stop when I got there, two boys and a girl. One of the boys was playing a Game Boy Advance, and he didn't even look up when I approached. The other two were busy talking, and they glanced in my direction and then looked away, continuing their conversation as if I didn't exist.

Welcome to Twin Lakes, New York.

I stood there, eavesdropping. I mean, what else did I have to do?

". . . seriously, I can't believe Kelly and Rick broke up over the summer. I thought they were going out for life."

"Yeah, well, absence doesn't always make the heart grow fonder, I guess."

I hoped that wasn't true. I thought about Roberto. His school in Miami had already started. If I were in Buenos Aires, I'd be excited to start school instead of nervous. Excited to see my friends. I would *have* friends, instead of feeling so strange and alone. Just overhearing about the breakup of this couple, Rick and Kelly, two people I didn't even know or care about, had me worrying about what would happen with Roberto.

Before I could completely depress myself, a large yellow bus pulled up, and I followed the other three onto it. I found an empty seat next to a girl who looked half asleep, and listened to the chatter around me, trying to make sense of it to distract myself from my gloomy thoughts.

When we pulled up at the high school, I followed the crowd into the gymnasium, where we were directed to tables according to the first initial of our last name. There, we lined up to get our schedules, and locker numbers and combinations.

When I got mine, it made no sense to me at all. It had a lot of numbers and letters and I was completely confused. I felt like sitting on the floor of the gymnasium and crying, but instead I went to find a teacher.

"*Por favor*, excuse me. It's my first day here and I don't know where I'm supposed to go."

The teacher took my schedule and locker number.

"Let's see . . . your locker is in Baker building. That's B building. Let me get someone whose locker is over there to show you the way."

He walked over to one of the tables and conferred with another teacher. A minute later he came back, accompanied by a shaggy-haired boy wearing a U2 T-shirt.

"This is Jake. Jake, this is . . ."

"Daniela."

"Jake, please show Daniela where her locker is over in B building. Make sure she can open it, too, okay?"

Jake nodded.

"C'mon," he said. "Let's boogie."

I wasn't sure what it meant to "boogie," but I followed him out of the gym.

"So, you're new?" he asked.

"Yes."

"Where are you from?"

"Argentina."

"Cool. Great soccer team."

True, but despite having gone out with Roberto, I wasn't football mad, so that was pretty much the end of that conversation.

"This is the crosswalk between Adams and Baker build-ing," Jake said, as we walked down a window-lined hallway. "You'll probably be using this quite a lot during the day. The gym, the media center, and the auditorium are in Adams. The cafeteria is in Baker."

We went up a flight of stairs and down a locker-lined hallway and finally Jake stopped.

"Here, this one's yours. Try opening it. It's not always easy."

I tried the combination and couldn't get the door open.

"Here, let me try."

Jake tried and couldn't open it, either. Finally he smashed the locker with his fist and the door popped open.

"It just takes the magic touch," he said with a smile.

"Maybe, but I'm not sure that I'm going to be able to do that when I need to open it again."

"These lockers suck. Don't ever leave anything of value in your locker anyway. Like if you have a cell phone or an iPod and you leave it there, it'll be gone, for sure."

I wished I could afford a cell phone or an iPod to put in my locker in the first place. If I had a cell phone, I could call Roberto. If I had an iPod, I could listen to music on the bus instead of fragments of other people's conversations that I had to work to understand.

"Where's your homeroom?" Jake asked. "If it's near here, I'll show you where it is."

I showed him my schedule and he noted the room, which luckily was just down the hallway on the left.

"So did you ever see that movie *Evita*? The one with Madonna? My parents got it on Netflix and made us watch it. I mean, it wasn't so bad, although musicals aren't really my thing, but that was about Argentina, wasn't it?"

I had no idea what he meant by "Netflix," but that movie had been all over the news in Argentina when they made it.

"Yes, it was. About Evita Perón. There were protests when the movie was filming because some people didn't want Madonna to play Evita," I told him.

"Seriously? Why not?"

"Well . . . for a lot of people in Argentina, Evita Perón was like a saint. And to have her played by this woman, you know, with the pointy bras and . . . well, they thought it was . . . how do you say in it English? *Degradante*."

I couldn't think of the word, but Jake seemed to get the point anyway.

"Do you think that?"

I didn't want him to think I was a prude.

"No. I'm just saying, it's what some people in Argentina thought."

"Wow. I didn't know that. I'll have to tell my parents tonight. Anyway, here's your homeroom. Good luck with your first day, Daniela."

"Thanks. I'm sure I'll need it."

*   *   *

Homeroom consisted of the teacher taking attendance and us having to fill in forms. It only lasted for half an hour, ten minutes of which were taken up by announcements that I could barely understand, which came over a crackly loudspeaker. I didn't worry too much about not understanding, though, because no one else even appeared to be listening.

Then the bell rang and we were told to go to our first-period class. I checked my schedule and it was Mathematics, in Room A104. A104. Where was that? All the classrooms in the building I was in began with B. Did that mean it was in the first building? It must. But how was I supposed to get back there? I had no idea how to get to my math class, and I didn't want to be late.

There was a group of girls at the end of the hall and even though I was nervous about approaching them, I didn't have much choice if I was going to make it to math class before lunchtime.

I stood next to them, waiting for them to say "hello" or "can I help you?" or "are you lost?" It was the first day of school, and the girls looked far too confident to be first-years. But they just ignored me.

"*Por favor*, uh, excuse me . . ."

Most of them kept on ignoring me, but one of them turned long enough to give me a quick glance. I was about to turn away when she said, "Wait! Where did you get that shirt?"

I felt fire rising in my cheeks and sweat gathering under my arms. It was my first day of a new school in a new country and the last thing I wanted to do is admit to a girl I didn't even know that everything I was wearing except for my underwear and shoes came from charity. So I ignored her and asked, "Can you tell me please how to get to room A104?"

She ignored me right back. "Jess, isn't that the shirt your dad got you in Monaco that time he went on business?"

The one she called Jess stopped talking and looked me over from head to toe with big brown eyes. She was really pretty. Her long dark hair curled just the right amount without frizzing and it was obvious that none of *her* clothes were from a charity. Oh no. Everything was the latest style and all her accessories matched to perfection.

It was clear from her expression that she didn't like what she saw.

"I think you're right, Coty. That *is* my shirt. I can't imagine that there are too many aquamarine Commes les Poissons shirts in this town." She shrugged her slim shoulders. "My mother must have had one of her charity clean outs for Jewish Family Services or something. I liked that shirt but, whatever. It just means I can guilt her into another shopping expedition — 'But, Mom, you gave away that shirt Dad bought me. . . .'"

If I hadn't been too embarrassed to be seen in just my bra on my first day of school, I'd have ripped off her stupid shirt and thrown it in her smirking face. Part of me wanted to punch her in the nose and another part wanted to crawl under a rock and die. But the biggest part of me wanted to be back in Argentina — if only that were possible.

Rather than stand there being humiliated, I decided to walk away and try to find someone else to give me directions to room A104.

My face was hot and my eyes were burning with tears of anger and shame as I hurried down the hallway, heading I wasn't sure where, and —

"Hey, watch where you're going!"

I had been so busy looking down at the floor trying not to cry that I walked right into some guy.

"*Excusa* — I mean, I'm sorry. I wasn't looking . . . I mean . . ."

"Are you okay? You look a little . . ."

I looked into the stranger's concerned eyes, and there was just enough of a hint of Roberto's in them that it sent me over the edge. I burst into tears.

"Hey, what's the matter? It can't be that bad," he said. I felt him patting my shoulder awkwardly, like he didn't really know what to do with this strange girl he'd never met who bumped into him and then started crying.

"Y-yes. It c-c-can," I hiccupped. "I c-c-an't find r-r-oom A104."

"Wow. Now that is a tragedy," he said. "But, you know, I think I might just be able to help you out with that."

He rooted around in the pocket of his shorts and handed me a tissue.

"Here. I think it's even mostly clean."

At that point I was more worried about running snot and mascara than germs, so I took it gratefully.

"Can you really help me find room A104?" I sniffed, wiping my eyes. "I think I'm going to be late and I don't want to get a detention."

"First of all, they won't give you a detention on the first day of school. Second of all, it's obvious you're new to the school, so you're doubly off the hook. And third of all . . . well, I can't think of a third of all. But don't worry. C'mon, this way."

He tapped my arm lightly and headed down the hall-way in the direction he came. Part of me wondered if he'd get in trouble for being late to wherever he was heading. The other part of me wondered what he meant by "off the hook."

"So where are you from?" he asked. "Clearly nowhere local."

"Argentina," I told him. "We moved here from Buenos Aires just over a month ago."

"So what's your name, Miss I'm-a-lost-girl-from-Argentina?"

"Daniela. Daniela Bensimon. But my friends call me Dani."

He pushed the door open into the stairwell. I followed him down the stairs.

"I'm Brian, by the way. Brian Harrison. So are you having a rough time adjusting?"

Talk about an understatement. Rough didn't even begin to describe how it felt at that point. But then I thought about how much rougher it could have been if Tío Jacobo hadn't helped us and we'd stayed in Argentina. "It's very different here, and with a new language and . . ."

"And getting lost trying to find your classroom," he said.

"And that."

And those girls making fun of me because I'm wearing clothes from Jewish Family Services . . .

"Okay, listen up. Remember this location. This is the connector corridor between Adams and Baker buildings, affectionately known as The Crosswalk. You will probably walk this something like five bazillion times a week between now and June."

"Bazillion?"

Brian laughed. "As in, lots and lots of times."

"Oh yes. I was here this morning once already with Jake."

"Jake Freheit?"

"I don't know."

"Longish hair, wearing a U2 shirt?"

"*Sí* — I mean, yes."

"He lives on my street and is one of my best buddies. So anyway, you'll probably be walking across here at least five more times today. Any classrooms that begin with an A are in Adams building, which is the one we're about to enter, and any ones that begin with B are in Baker, which is the building we just left."

"Which is where my locker and my homeroom are."

"Right. So you'll need to figure out which books to take with you in the morning because you won't always have time to run back to your locker between classes. Unless you're a really quick sprinter, in which case I'd really love you to try out for the track team, because we could do with some good sprinters."

I thought about my limited athletic skills and laughed. "I'm probably the last person you would want on your track team. Unless you really wanted to lose."

"So, just out of curiosity, because I'm a curious kind of guy, what kind of team would I want you on?"

Good question. We walked in silence down the noisy corridor for a moment, Brian saying, "What's up?" and "Hey, how was your summer?" as we passed by people, but without really stopping to listen to the answers.

"I suppose your speaks-fluent-Spanish-and-a-bit-of-Hebrew team. Or maybe your makes-pretty-good-*pasteles*-and-*alfajores* team."

"I don't know what *pasteles* and *alfajores* are, but if they're edible, then I definitely want you on my team."

I laughed. "*Pasteles* are a pastry filled with caramel and *alfajores* are two cookies stuck together with *dulce de leche*. They're both delicious."

"Well, Ms. International Food Network, I am really pleased that I bumped into you, because I'm hoping that maybe someday my Good Samaritan actions might earn me a taste of some of your amazing Argentinean cookies. But in any event, here you are at Room A104. And from now on, if you're lost, ask me for directions. You can think of me as your personal GPS."

He gave me a crooked, offbeat smile, and even though he wasn't typically handsome like Roberto, at that moment I found him attractive.

"Thanks, GPS — er, Brian," I said, and headed into my math class with a sigh of relief. At least numbers are the same in every language.

After Math, my next class was "Language Arts." Thankfully, it was in an "A" classroom. But I wasn't sure what "Language Arts" meant. Was it an art class or a language class? I knew it wasn't ESL or "English as a Second Language," because I had that later. I used to think I understood English passably well until I came to Twin Lakes and had to navigate my way around school.

The hallway was as noisy and frightening as before, but I managed to find room A203 without bumping into those girls.

I found a seat near the front but not too close to it, next to a boy who was writing in a bound notebook. Even though there were other empty seats, I chose him to sit next to because he was the only person in the room who wasn't already engaged in lively conversation, maybe because everyone was ignoring him.

He glanced at me briefly, but didn't say anything; he just turned his attention back to his notebook.

Estupendo. I was being ignored by the guy everyone else was ignoring. I sat at my desk, swallowing hard so I didn't cry, and tried to remember that I was once a person who had friends. I opened my notebook to the back and wrote in small letters: ROBERTO, GABY, SOFIA, RICARDO, MILI, LEO, DAVID . . . names of people I wished were sitting in the chairs next to me. Names of people I'd probably never see again. Ever.

Just when I thought I was going to drown in misery, the bell rang.

"Settle down, people," the teacher said.

Settle down? I jotted the phrase down in my notebook to ask the ESL teacher.

The Language Arts teacher's name was Mr. Hallowell, and like every other teacher, he took attendance.

Like every other teacher he mispronounced my name Ben-simon.

"It's Ben-*simone*," I told him.

I heard someone in the back of class imitating me saying Bensimon and I felt my cheeks flush.

"Oh, you're the new student from Chile, right?"

"No, Argentina."

"Close, though." He smiled.

Not that close.

"Actually, Santiago, the capital of Chile, is just over seven hundred miles from Buenos Aires, the capital of Argentina," said the kid with the notebook. "That's eleven hundred kilometers."

Where did that *come from? How does he* know *that?*

Everyone turned to stare at him, including Mr. Hallowell.

"Is that right, Mr. . . . ?"

He looked at his attendance sheet as if it would miraculously reveal Geography Boy's name.

"Argentina is almost double the size in terms of square miles occupied. It's a much bigger country," Geography Boy continued, seemingly unaware that a) the teacher was waiting for his name or b) the entire class was staring at him like he was a fact-spouting freak.

"That's very interesting, but right now I'd like to know your name."

"Jon Nathanson."

There was whispering going on all around me.

"That's enough, class. Mr. Nathanson, this is all fascinating information but not relevant to the taking of attendance, so I'm going to have to ask you to save it for another time."

The people in the class snickered. Jon lowered his head and started writing in his notebook again. I felt sorry for him. He might have been born in America, but in that classroom it was clear he was almost as much of an outsider as I was.

Language Arts, it turned out, was literature. We were going to start off by reading *Hamlet*. *Perfecto*. Not only did I have to learn in a language I wasn't 100 percent fluent in, I had to read a play written in a form of that language several centuries old. I wondered if they would let me read it in Spanish. I mean, seriously. Otherwise it was like asking me to run a marathon with my legs tied together, carrying a concrete block.

When the bell rang at the end of class, I turned to Jon, who was busy putting his books in his backpack, and tapped him on the shoulder. He jumped, like he wasn't used to people touching him.

"Sorry . . . I just . . . how did you know so much about my country?" I asked him. "I couldn't tell you the exact distance between Santiago and Buenos Aires, and I've lived in Buenos Aires my entire life."

"Until now," he said.

"Well, yes, until about a month ago, to be precise." We walked to the classroom door together. "So, how did you know all that?"

"I like facts," he said. "I like to read books and visit websites that have facts. And I've got a really good memory."

"You must, to remember that kind of detail. Remind me to have you on my team if there's ever a trivia quiz. I'm Dani, by the way."

I took my schedule out of my notebook. Lunch next.

"Could you tell me how to get to the cafeteria?"

"I have lunch, too — I can take you there if you want," he said.

"*Gracias* — I mean, thank you. I keep getting lost in the hallways, and people were . . ."

I stopped, because I didn't want to tell him about the incident with those girls.

"Yeah, the hallways can be rough. I try to spend as little time in them as I can."

I guess it was the same for all of us *tipos raros*. The corridors at school were dangerous terrain.

When we got to the cafeteria my heart sank, because standing right in front of us in the line for food were my tormentors. After the way they humiliated me about my clothes, the last thing I needed was for them to see that I had vouchers to pay for my lunch. It would be yet another nail in my Poor Girl coffin. But I couldn't just walk away from Jon. He was busy telling me every fact he knew about Argentina, and believe me, there were plenty, including a few that I didn't know, and which at any other time I'd have found really interesting. If he'd only taken a breath, I could have pretended that I had to go to the WC, but he just went on and on, seemingly oblivious to my growing tension.

"Hey, Jon-boy," said the worst girl, the one they called Jess, smiling at my companion. She ignored me. I couldn't believe she was paying attention to Geography Boy. He seemed like the kind of guy who'd be beneath her notice. I worried that she was just being nice so she could humiliate him later. But strangely, she looked genuinely pleased to see him.

"Hi, Jess," Jon said. "This is Dani. She's from Argentina."

"Really? How interesting." The way Jess said "interesting" made it sound the complete opposite. I wondered why she seemed to hate me so much already. Was it because I was wearing her old clothes or because I was an *extranjera*?

Jess linked her arm through Jon's, effectively turning her back on me. "So how's your day going?"

I watched Jess's friends, to see if they were secretly snickering while she made fun of my unusual friend, but they acted as if the sight of her being arm and arm with Jon was perfectly natural. *He can't possibly be her boyfriend. There's no way.*

Then I overheard her reminding him, "And don't forget, Mom is picking us up today, so don't get on the bus."

So that's it. She's his sister. I didn't realize how intently I was looking at them, searching for a family resemblance, until Jess turned around at the lunch checkout and said, "What are you staring at, Argentina?"

Her eyes fell to the lunch voucher in my hand and I waited for her to say something, but she didn't. She just laughed. And somehow, that was worse than words.

I ate lunch by myself, praying for the rest of the day to be over so I could go home. The problem was, I knew I'd have to go back tomorrow. And the next day. And the day after that.

That evening, Sarita was full of stories about school. Clearly getting lost and meeting horrible girls wasn't a part of *her* first-day-of-school experience.

"My teacher, Mrs. Jordan, is really nice and she's so pretty, much prettier than Señora Silva, but then she's much younger, too. Señora Silva was old. I like having a young teacher, don't you? Did you make any new friends today, Dani? I've already made two new friends, Linley and Emma. They're really fun. We played this game called Tag and another one called Duck, Duck, Goose. Isn't that a funny name? You sit in a circle and . . ."

It didn't take long for Papá to explode.

"Enough, Sarita! Can I at least have five minutes of peace and quiet to eat and digest my meal without your constant talking?"

Sarita lowered her head as tears welled in her eyes.

Mamá sighed and she grasped Sari's hand under the table.

"Come, *preciosa*, eat your dinner and then afterward, you can tell us all about school and about this strange game, what was it? Chicken, Chicken, Duck?"

Mamá knew exactly what Sari said, but she'd grown expert at trying to diffuse the tension between Papá and the rest of us.

"No, Mamá," Sari sniffed. "Duck, Duck, Goose."

She took her fork and started to eat, but I was seething, so filled with fury that I had no room left for food. Why? Why did Papá continue to behave this way? Why did we have to put up with it?

I knew things were hard for Papá, and I tried to be understanding and sympathetic, but inside I was screaming, *What about me?* I'd had an awful first day of school and I wanted to be able to tell my parents about it, to have them listen and give me some advice or to just say, *Poor Dani, we know this is hard for you, but don't worry, we know things will get better.*

But instead I sat swallowing what I was feeling like it was the bitterest of medicines, the taste of it practically choking me.

"Dani, why aren't you eating?" Mamá asked.

I took a deep breath and tried to absorb the rest of my rage. There was no point lashing out at Mamá. Things were hard enough for her, trying to navigate us all through the storms of Papá's moods.

"It's nothing." I picked up my knife and fork and took a bite of food. Despite the fact that I'd cooked supper, I couldn't have told you what I was eating. It all tasted like anger.

"How was your first day of school?" Mamá asked.

I took another bite and wondered for a second how it would feel if I were to tell them the truth about my day. But only for second. I looked into Mamá's tired eyes and knew that I wouldn't.

"It was fine. I got lost a few times. It's hard to find your way around."

"I'm glad my school isn't that big," Sarita said. "I'm glad it's a long time before I have to go to high school. I'm too scared to go there."

"Well, by the time you have to go to high school, it won't seem so big," Mamá told her. "And you won't be scared to go there."

If only that were true — because I was terrified to have to go back the next day.

Chapter Nine

$\mathcal{T}$HE KIDS AT THE BUS STOP at least nodded to acknowledge me the next morning, although no one spoke. I managed to find my way to my locker, and open it. Being in classes was hard, but the worst part was getting there — navigating my way through the crowded, noisy hallways, trying to figure out if I was in the right building and if I had the correct books with me, and most of all trying to avoid bumping into *those girls*.

History class. Found the room. Found a seat. I was even a minute early, so I could relax.

"Hey, Evita."

The tap on my shoulder was a clue that "Evita" meant me. I turned around to see that guy from yesterday, the one who rescued me when I was lost. I didn't realize he was in my class. Why did it seem that what little people knew about my country — well, except for Jon, but he was clearly a special case — they seemed to have learned from the movie *Evita*? Didn't they teach geography in America?

"Oh, hello. It's my GPS. I'm afraid I've forgotten your name — and you've obviously forgotten mine."

"Actually, I haven't. Daniela 'But My Friends Call Me Dani' Bensimon."

Now who felt like an *idiota*?

"Okay, Personal GPS, but I really *have* forgotten yours."

He grimaced and placed his hands over his heart in mock agony.

"You really know how to hurt a guy, Evita," he said, pretending to fall off his chair onto the floor. "I'm crushed. Completely crushed."

"Well, why don't you get up and tell me your name instead of cleaning the floor with your jeans?"

He grinned suddenly, and it transformed his face. The realization that he was handsome shot an unwelcome tingle down my spine. *Roberto. Mi novio es Roberto,* I reminded myself sternly.

GPS held out his hand for assistance, and I stood to grasp it and pull him to his feet. He was taller than Roberto — when he was standing I only came up to his shoulder.

"The name is Brian. Brian Harrison," he said, shaking my hand, which was still firmly retained in his grasp. "That's B-R-I-A-N H-A-R-R-I-S-O-N. Try to remember it this time, okay? Otherwise I might have to resort to more desperate measures to imprint myself in your memory." He grinned. "And we wouldn't want that, would we?"

His smile reignited the spine tingle, and I was suddenly not so sure I wouldn't want it. I pulled my hand out of his grasp and turned to sit down at my desk.

"Brian Harrison. I'll write it down so I remember."

I felt consumed by guilt. If I was feeling spine tingles for Brian Harrison, did that mean Roberto might have similar feelings for some girl down in Miami? I wanted to race to the library to IM Roberto, to ask him if there was anyone else, if he still loved me. But it was time for class.

I found it hard to concentrate while the teacher was lecturing; I kept writing Roberto's name in tiny letters in the margin of my notebook. I needed to contact him. I desperately wanted to hear his voice. Maybe I could beg Mamá to let me call him, even just for five minutes. But with money being so tight, spending on long distance calls to my boyfriend was pretty far down the family priority list. Anyway, I didn't even know his phone number.

After class, Brian walked with me down the hallway.

"So do your parents talk about what it was like living in Argentina during the Dirty War?" he asked. "Like, did anyone in your family get Disappeared?"

I stopped and looked at him, shocked. In Argentina, one just didn't come out and ask such a thing. My parents still only talked about the Disappearances in hushed tones.

"I'm sorry — did I say something wrong?"

He took off his sneaker and opened his mouth wide.

"Open mouth and insert foot. That's a Brian Harrison specialty."

I had no idea what he was talking about, and my confusion obviously showed on my face.

"It's an expression. To put your foot in your mouth means to say something stupid and tactless that you shouldn't have said. You know, that offends the other person."

"Oh . . . now I understand. An idiom."

"Yes. In this case an idiom used by an idiot. I'm sorry."

"I have a problem with idioms," I told him. "I didn't learn them all at school."

"Some of them can be pretty colorful," Brian said. "I'll have to teach you — that's if you'll still talk to me after I put my foot in my mouth."

He took a pretend bite out of his sneaker before sliding it back on his foot.

I laughed.

"I suppose I can still talk to you. Otherwise, how will I find my way to my next class?"

"True. You are one smart cookie, Miss Daniela Bensimon from Argentina. Come on, tell me where's your next class and I'll show you the way."

As I told him the classroom number of my next class, I

tried to figure out why he was comparing me to a biscuit, and if this was a compliment or an insult. It was no wonder I felt so tired at the end of the day. Trying to think in English was exhausting.

"Hey? How's it going? Daniela, right?"

I was walking to the bus and saw Jake, the guy who'd shown me to my locker on my first day of school.

"Oh, hi. You can call me Dani. And things are going . . . okay, I guess."

"My buddy Brian said he'd bumped into you."

"Brian Harrison?"

Jake nodded.

"Actually, I think I was the one who bumped into him."

Jake laughed.

"Good one. So listen, I'm a member of the Twin Lakes Players, and I was thinking you should try out for the play we're doing. There's a part you'd be great for. I told the director I met you on the first day of school and he said you should definitely come to the auditions."

"I . . . well . . . I don't know. I've never . . ."

"It's fun. Seriously. And you'd meet people. I'd introduce you to everyone. Tryouts are after school this Thursday."

After school. When I was supposed to be at home, looking after Sarita.

"*Ciertamente.* I'll think about it."

"Cool. See ya!"

The whole bus ride home I was thinking about trying out for a play, imagining myself on stage, being a part of something, and best of all, having something to look forward to besides going to school and coming home to the apartment where Papá's depression cast a pall over everything.

But when I told Mamá as we washed the dishes after dinner, she sat me down at the kitchen table and looked at me sadly.

"Dani, I would love for you to be able to do this, but at the moment I'm counting on you to look after your sister in the afternoons until I get home from work. Maybe eventually when . . ."

She wouldn't say it, but I knew what she meant. When we could finally rely on Papá again.

"But it's not fair, Mamá. I . . ."

I couldn't say more because it looked like Mamá was about to cry, and I didn't want to be the one responsible for her tears.

I stormed out of the kitchen, but I was so angry when I went to my room that it was hard to stay still or concentrate on anything. Just because Papá had put his life on hold, why did I have to put mine on hold, too?

I needed to get out. I wanted to be with my friends. Since I didn't have any good friends in Twin Lakes, that meant going online, and since we couldn't afford a computer of our own, that meant a trip to the library.

Slinging my backpack onto my shoulder, I walked back into the kitchen. "I'm going to walk to the library. I need to do some research for school."

"Now?" Mamá said. "But it's late. . . ."

"The library is open until nine o'clock. I'll be fine. It's safe here."

"Take some quarters and call here when you're finished. Papá will come to walk you home."

Perfecto. Here I was trying to get away from home, from everything to do with Papá, and now I was going to be stuck walking home with him?

"He doesn't need to. I can walk back by myself."

"Dani, if you want to go to the library, Papá is going to walk you home."

"But, Mamá . . ."

"Enough, Daniela," Papá growled from the living room. "Listen to your mother."

My eyes began to prickle with tears of anger and frustration.

"Okay, okay, I'll call. *Hasta luego.*"

I stalked out of the apartment, not quite slamming the door, but shutting it harder than usual.

It was a beautiful evening. It had cooled off from the intense heat of the day, and a breeze rustled the leaves on the trees that lined our street. The tips of some were starting to turn yellow, just a hint of autumn, which was strange for me to see in early September: a reminder that I was no longer in the Southern Hemisphere. I just wished I were walking down the street hand in hand with Roberto, instead of by myself. Or arm in arm with Gaby, talking about anything and everything, the way we always did. I tried to calculate the time difference between the United States and Israel — Gaby would be asleep for certain by the time I got to the library. I just hoped that I caught Beto online. I missed him so much.

Fortunately, I didn't have to wait for a computer. I logged onto MSN and felt a rush of joy when I saw that Beto was logged in, too.

Hola querido!

Hola!

Miss U.

Miss U2!

Miss U more!

How r things?

OK I guess.

I wanted so much to talk to someone about how things were, about how angry I was at my father for not doing anything to get better, about how unfair life seemed. If it had been Gaby, maybe I would have, but I spoke to Beto so rarely, I didn't want him to think all I did was complain.

What's your new school like?

HUGE!

Mine too.

I need a GPS just to find my way around.

As I clicked SEND, I thought of Brian Harrison, my personal GPS, and the spine tingles he caused. My face flushed with guilt, and I quickly pushed him out of my mind and focused my thoughts back on Beto.

LOL.

How are things in Miami?

Good. School is easy. Nice beach. Pretty girls. JOKE!

I hoped it was a joke. I wished it were a joke he hadn't made, because all I could think about was Beto on the beach surrounded by pretty girls. It wasn't a pleasant image.

Ha-ha. Not funny.

Made friends yet?

Had I? I guess Jon. Sort of. And Brian. And there was a nice girl in my ESL class, Rosalia.

One or two. What about you?

Quite a few. But I've been here longer than you've been there. Give yourself time.

I suppose.

I kept seeing him on the beach surrounded by girls in bikinis. Stop, brain. Stop.

I've got to go — my dad needs to use the computer.

No! Not yet . . .

Let's talk again soon, OK?

K. Miss you.

Miss you 2.

xoxoxoxo

xoxoxo bye

I stared at the blinking cursor after he signed off, feeling bereft. If only I had the money to call him, to hear his voice. If only I could get on a plane and fly to Miami, to see his smile and feel his arms around me. If only I didn't have to watch Sarita after school, I could get a job and earn money to pay for a cell phone so I could call Roberto when I wanted. It was all so unfair.

I didn't want to go home, so I wrote a long e-mail to Gaby telling her all about Jon and Brian GPS and horrible Jessica and how hard things were at home. Then I sat around Googling Miami until they announced that the library was closing in fifteen minutes, at which point I called my father to come pick me up.

By the time he got to the library, the parking lot was almost deserted and I had to admit it was a little frightening.

"Come, let's get you home," Papá said.

We walked back to the apartment in silence. There was so much I wanted to say to my father — so much had been building up inside me that I'd swallowed like a bitter pill. Sometimes I could feel it festering inside me, corroding parts of my deepest self until it felt like I was no longer a stable structure. But it was more than I could do to open my mouth to speak. I was too afraid. Afraid of the consequences, of how he might react. But also of what I might say if I finally let the words out.

I thought about other walks I'd taken with my father, walks we took Before. We'd walk for what seemed like miles in the sunshine, my little hand held in his bigger one, and I had thought that there was no man more handsome, more intelligent, more kind, more wonderful than my *papá*.

I wished I could summon up some of those feelings.

"Your school, it is good?" he said finally, as if the silence was too much for him.

"It's okay so far. It's just very big. I get lost trying to find my classes."

There was so much more I could tell him. I was sure he would understand how humiliated I felt when that girl Jessica looked down at me on the first day of school because I was wearing her cast-off clothes. But then he would say, "I told you we shouldn't take charity," or something like that. Or maybe he'd make us give all of the clothes back to Mrs. Ehrenkranz, and Sarita would be devastated. So I kept those feelings with all the other unsaid words that festered inside.

"I'm sure you'll learn your way around soon," Papá said.

But will I ever learn my way back to you?

"Yes, I'm sure you're right. It'll just take a little while."

We walked the rest of the way home in silence, each of us trapped in our own thoughts.

Chapter Ten

I ONLY GOT LOST a few more times over the next week. One teacher, Mrs. Savarin, gave me a warning for being late, but I think she realized that I wasn't like those kids Derek and Trevor who messed around in the hallways and ended up being late for class, so she held off from giving me a detention, which was a huge relief. The thought of having to explain to my parents that I was late coming home from school because of a detention filled me with terror.

Still, it was a pretty lonely existence I led at Twin Lakes High. I hadn't made many friends, except for Rosalia and Jon. Jon sat with me at lunch most days, because we'd walk down to the cafeteria together right after Language Arts.

There was something different about him. He rarely looked me in the eye when he spoke to me, and he walked awkwardly, his shoulders hunched over as if he were permanently tense. But he was incredibly smart. And he had a phenomenal memory for facts; having a discussion with him was like talking to a living encyclopedia. Jon seemed to know some fact about every subject I ever discussed with him, whether it was sports, geography, the environment, art, or even current events topics like the War on Terror.

But it was strange the way he had problems with phrases, the same way I did, even though English was his native language. Like the time we were having lunch and I accidentally knocked over my milk carton. Jon handed me a napkin and said, "No use crying over spilled milk," and then he started laughing and laughing. I stared at him, confused, because I wasn't crying. Not even close.

I mopped up my spill, and then asked, "Jon — I don't understand. What's so funny?"

He told me that "No use crying over spilled milk" was an expression, meaning that you shouldn't get upset or angry after something has gone wrong because it can't be changed. *Maybe I should teach that one to Papá,* I thought.

Jon told me when he was younger he had a hard time understanding idioms, too. His parents, his teachers, and even his sister, Evil Jessica, had to explain the meanings to him.

"I remember the first time my mom told us we couldn't go to the park because it was 'raining cats and dogs,'" Jon said. "I ran to the window expecting to see Labradors and Siamese cats falling from the skies. I was so disappointed when it was just boring old rain."

The thought of Jon standing by the window waiting for dogs and cats to rain down from the heavens made me burst out laughing.

"You think that's funny. . . . Once Mom was talking to Dad about our aunt Marilyn and how she always 'wears her heart on her sleeve' . . ."

"What?!"

"Well, yeah, that's what I thought. I was only six at the time, and the next time Aunt Marilyn came over I was standing next to her staring at her arm. Eventually, she asked me what I was doing, and I told her I was looking for her heart because Mom said she wore it on her sleeve. You can imagine how embarrassed Mom was — Dad was trying really hard not to laugh, but Aunt Marilyn got mad. Dad told me later that it wasn't my fault, and that what Mom meant is that Aunt Marilyn tends to be open about how she's feeling."

In the Bensimon household one did not "wear one's heart on one's sleeve," that was for sure.

"I'm going to have to write these down," I told Jon. "You have to teach me expressions like this, so I sound like a proper American."

"A real American. A real American wouldn't say 'proper.'"

"Okay, a *real* American."

The Evil Jessica and two of her followers came over just as we were clearing away our lunch debris. "Hey, Jon-boy, don't forget, we're taking the bus home today, okay? I'll meet you out front by the flagpole."

"Sure, okay. See you there."

They completely ignored my existence.

I wondered how the same family could produce someone as nice as Jon and as horrible as his sister. Well, Lucrezia Borgia probably had at least one nice brother, too.

Jon was never without the notebook he was drawing in the first day I met him, and he was always scribbling in it. To use an idiom he taught me, he was always "buried in a book" — that particular book, to be precise. I wanted so much to know what he was writing in there, but didn't feel like I could ask him. Maybe one day, when I knew him better. Until then, I'd just have to wonder.

Brian, my personal GPS, talked to me every day in History, and then walked me to my next class. He was always asking me questions about life in Argentina. I got the impression that he went home and did research every night so he could ask me more questions the following day. Like, one day, he asked me about why we ended up moving to the United States and I told him a little bit about the Crisis (leaving out everything about Papá losing his business and becoming . . . well, the way he was), and the next day we were walking down the hallway and Brian suddenly asked me about the *cacerolazos*. I laughed at his pronunciation, but couldn't imagine that he'd heard about that on the news all the way in Twin Lakes, New York, so he must have been looking stuff up online since we spoke the day before. I told him how people took to the streets, banging on pots and pans in protest because they couldn't take their own money out of the bank. Not that it did any good.

I didn't tell Brian that any of this happened to my family. But from the look he gave me with his deep brown eyes, and the way he touched my arm and said, "That must have been awful, Dani," I think he knew.

One day, I was walking down the hall with Rosalia after ESL, speaking in Spanish. I knew I should have been practicing my English with her, but it was just so hard to be constantly thinking in another language — to be able to be myself in my own mother tongue felt . . . I don't know . . . restful. When I had to speak English it was like I had to think on two levels — what we were speaking about in the conversation, and the actual language of how I was going to say it. In Spanish, the language part was second nature, so I could just say what I meant without worrying that it would come out meaning something else.

Anyway, we were chatting away when I heard someone behind us say very loudly, "These foreigners — if they're going to come to our country, the least they can do is make the effort to learn our language."

I didn't want to turn around, but Rosalia spun angrily to face the speaker. It was Trevor, the perpetually late guy from my science class. Standing next to him, smirking, was his friend Derek.

"I speak two languages better than you speak one, *imbécil*," Rosalia said.

"Oh, go back to where you came from, bitch," Trevor said. "I bet you're here illegally anyway."

"Yeah, it's people like you who caused 9/11," Derek chimed in. "They should just build a wall high enough to keep all of you guys out."

I couldn't believe what I was hearing. Did these boys seriously think people like Rosalia and me were capable of doing the awful things that happened on September 11? That we could kill all those innocent people?

My heart was thumping against the wall of my chest, so loudly I could hear it in my ears, and I realized my hands were clenched into fists.

"How DARE you say that! My aunt was killed by terrorists in Argentina. If you think I could inflict that kind of suffering on anyone else, you are . . . well, you are just . . ."

I was so upset I couldn't think of anything bad enough to call him.

"Whoa," Trevor said. "I didn't know that."

How could he not know? It was such a major part of my life, looming like a dark cloud over my family ever since it happened. It was hard for me to believe that there were people in the world who didn't know what happened on July 18, 1994.

"I could write a *book* about all the things you don't know," sniffed Rosalia.

"Was it Al-Qaeda?" Derek asked.

"No, it wasn't Al-Qaeda," I told him. Why did Americans assume that every act of terrorism was Al-Qaeda, just because that was who was behind the attacks on September 11? "They never proved for sure who did it. They think it was Hezbollah, with the help of the Iranians."

"Far out," Trevor said.

Far out? It wasn't far out. It was close to my heart, deeply personal.

"And for your information, both of us are here legally, so from now on you can keep your big traps shut!" Rosalia said, and grabbing my arm, she dragged me down the hall.

"I can't believe those *idiotas*," she fumed. "Where do they get the right to tell us to go home? We have our papers. We have every right to be here. What about *'Give me your tired, your poor, your huddled masses yearning to breathe free'*? It's engraved on the Statue of Liberty. That's supposed to be what America is about, isn't it?"

"Maybe not anymore. Maybe not after what happened."

"What, just because some terrorist fanatics did something evil, now we are all suspect? Where is the fairness in that?"

I stopped and looked at her. "Rosalia, *chica*, where is the fairness in anything?"

She sighed. "I suppose you're right, Dani, though I hate to admit it."

"So, Rosalia, I have a question."

"Yes, *chica*?"

"When you told Trevor and Derek, '*Keep your big traps shut*,' what exactly did you mean?"

Rosalia laughed.

"'Trap' is slang for mouth. So it means they should keep their big mouths shut. To shut up, in other words."

"'*Keep your big trap shut.*' I'll have to remember that one. I'm sure it will become useful."

Little did I realize just how soon that would be true.

Two days later I was waiting to pay with my coupons in the lunch line when, to my dismay, Evil Jessica and her gang joined the line behind me. Even Trevor and Derek would be preferable to the Evil J, because the clothes I was wearing were from the JFS bag, so they were probably hers. The last thing that I needed was another run down of my hand-me-down wardrobe. For her to see me paying with lunch vouchers was just added humiliation.

"Oh look, Jess, it's that girl again and she's wearing your old Seven jeans and that T-shirt I always liked. I wish your mom had given it to *me* instead of charity. Maybe I should tell her I'm poor or something."

Loud giggles from the Gang. I felt my face starting to flush bright red, but I just stared down at the tuna sandwich and yogurt on my lunch tray and tried very hard to ignore them.

"Oh right, as if, Cindy! Your father drives a Porsche for heaven's sake! I hardly think that qualifies you for hand-outs from Goodwill," said one of the girls.

"Yes, Coty, but it's a two-year-old Porsche. I should at least get food stamps or something, don't you think?"

More giggles.

I wanted so much to ignore them, to pretend that I didn't hear the things they were saying. But it made me angry that they could joke about poverty when it had changed my family's existence so completely over the last two years, so angry that I felt like I would explode if I didn't open my lips and say something. I kept staring down at my tray, but everything was becoming blurry.

"Why don't we ask this girl here about qualifying for food stamps?" came Jessica's bored voice. "After all, it's obvious from the lunch vouchers in her hand that she knows about them."

I didn't know if that overwhelming rage was what Papá felt when he exploded at us at home, but whatever it was, I could no longer contain it.

"Just shut your big trap!" I shouted, turning to Jessica and for once, looking her in the eye. "Shut up! Keep your big trap shut and leave me alone!"

People stared at me, but I was beyond caring.

Jessica met my gaze for a second, then shrugged and looked away.

"Whatever. Keep your hair on."

I was afraid to touch my hair to make sure it was still there in front of her, but I wondered if the force of my rage had caused it to shoot from the top of my head or burst into spontaneous flames. I was so angry that nothing would have surprised me.

I turned my back on Jessica and her friends, but made a mental note to ask Jon what "keep your hair on" meant.

Brian Harrison caught up to me as I walked to the bus that afternoon.

"Hey, Evita, what's the matter? You look like you have the weight of the world on your shoulders."

The weight of the world on your shoulders. I hadn't heard that expression before, but unlike a lot of things in English, it made perfect sense. It was how Mamá looked when she came home from work in the evenings. It described exactly how I was feeling as I walked to the bus, recalling the incident with Jessica and her friends in the cafeteria, and my reaction. How the rage and humiliation welled up inside me until I saw red behind the whites of my eyes and I wanted to throw my lunch tray in their smirking faces. How I was scared that maybe I was more like Papá than I knew, that even though I despised him for his moods and angry rages, maybe I was just the same as him.

"I've ... I guess you could say that I've had a bad day."

"Don't tell me you're still getting lost. I'll be offended if you got a detention for being late because you didn't utilize the services of your Personal GPS."

He actually managed to extract a tight smile from me.

"No, you've trained me well, Mr. GPS. It was just a . . . how do I say it? An unpleasant incident."

Brian was serious, suddenly.

"Who was it? Tell me, and I'll beat the crap out of him."

It cheered me slightly, knowing that Brian was willing to stick up for me.

"Actually, it was a 'her.' Several girls, if you want to know the truth."

Brian lifted up his hands in a gesture of surrender.

"Sorry, honey, you're on your own there. I'm an equal rights kinda guy, but it doesn't extend to punching out girls."

"I'm happy to hear that."

"So what was it about?" he asked.

I felt my face flushing as the humiliation of the lunch line came back to haunt me. Brian seemed to like me as I was, Dani the Girl from Argentina. I didn't want him to think of me as Poor Girl Dani.

Brian bent down and started to untie his shoelaces.

"What are you doing?" I asked.

He looked up at me with that grin of his.

"Well, it looks like I might have just put my foot in my mouth again, so I'm just getting prepared."

That made me laugh for real. He retied his laces and stood up, smiling.

"That's more like it," Brian said. Then he touched my arm and was serious again. "Look, I don't know what all of this was about, but I know some of the girls in this school can be mean. In fact, some of them can be downright bitches if you'll excuse the language. But try not to let them get you down. You're worth twenty of them."

I felt myself blushing.

"Thanks, but . . ."

"Seriously, Dani. Don't listen to them. Keep your chin up, as they say."

"What?"

"It means keep your head held high when people are trying to make you feel bad or the going gets tough."

What happens when you are tired of having to keep your chin up? I wondered. *What happens when you just want to rest your chin on someone's shoulder, to feel their arms around you and hear them say,* Dani, don't worry, everything is going to turn out okay?

"Keep my chin up," I repeated. "Yes, sir."

I looked at my watch and realized that I was going to be late for my bus.

"I have to go — I'm going to miss the bus."

"Okay, well, don't forget, chin up and smile! Because you're exceptionally pretty when you smile." He grinned. "See you tomorrow."

He walked off toward the student parking lot, and I stood there frozen for the few seconds it took me to absorb that Brian Harrison had just told me I was exceptionally pretty when I smiled. Then I ran to the bus, and arrived there breathless.

Chapter Eleven

MAMÁ LET ME BUY a small notebook that came with a tiny pencil so that I could carry it around in my pocket and write down words that I didn't know, or expressions for which I needed to ask the meaning. It filled up fast, with things like "Close but no cigar," which means that you came very close to accomplishing a goal but didn't quite make it. Or funny ones, like "When pigs fly," which means something that will never happen, and completely gruesome ones, like "It costs an arm and a leg," which means something is really expensive.

One thing was clear to me — English was a very strange language. I would go to sleep with my head so crammed with new words and expressions that my dreams were filled with flying pigs and rainstorms of cats and dogs. I wondered if I would ever be fluent, really fluent, like I was in Spanish. Sometimes, though, I'd catch myself thinking in English instead of Spanish. Señora Owen, my English teacher in Buenos Aires, always said that thinking in another language is a sign of fluency, so I figured there was hope. But so many times I found myself frustrated, trying to think about how to say something, worrying if the words that left my mouth were the ones that actually expressed what I was trying to say. And sometimes, after the words came out, people would look at me strangely or start laughing, and I'd know that those words weren't the right ones, or I'd pronounced them incorrectly, and I'd wish for the nine hundredth time that day that I was back in Argentina, speaking in my native tongue.

I hadn't managed to IM Roberto in a few weeks. We never seemed to be online at the same time. I'd send him long e-mails about Twin Lakes, about Jon, about Evil Jess, about everything that was happening in my life except for my conversations with Brian Harrison and what was happening at home. The e-mails he sent me back were short: "Hola, *just got back from the beach, hope you are making new friends, miss you, R xo*" or "*Guess what — we won our football (ha! Not soccer ☺) match 4–1 and guess who was the lead scorer? Hope all is well with you* — Besos, *Beto xoxo.*"

I was scared that he was slipping away from me, that his e-mails would get shorter and shorter until finally he stopped writing to me at all. And if that happened . . . I didn't want to think about losing Roberto, about not feeling like he was somewhere in America, loving me.

At least Gaby was still writing to me regularly.

Dani —

Shalom, chica! Greetings from Tel Aviv, where we have finally ended up after leaving the absorption center. Papá is going to be working in one of the hospitals here. Tel Aviv is cool — very modern and bustling and the beach is fantastic. You have these ultramodern high-rise hotels and then the Carmel market with all the fruits and spices and coffee roasters.

For all that Tel Aviv has so much going on, I miss the absorption center at Ra'anana. I'd made a lot of friends there, and we were all in the same boat. Here I'm much more conscious of being an extranjera *— like when I get a strange look and I know what I meant to say in Hebrew just came out really wrong or I've made a grammar mistake that a three-year-old would know better than to say. The teachers at school recommend that our family try to continue speaking Hebrew when we get home, but most times by the end of the day my brain hurts from having to think about what I'm saying all the time, and I just need to be able to open my mouth without having to plan out the sentence first.*

I'm sorry to hear things aren't so good at home. Do they provide any immigrant counseling in America? It's such an enormous change for anyone. Maybe it's just going to take your dad a little longer to adjust than it does for other people.

I miss you so much, Dani!! I heard about this new

program called Birthright Israel, where when you are eighteen you can get a free trip to visit Israel for ten days. I know it's a few years away, but you should look into it. You seem so far away from me, but I'd be happier if I knew we'd at least see each other again, sometime.

Give your parents my love and give Sari a big hug.
xoxo Gaby

I looked up Birthright Israel on the Internet, and Gaby was right. It was amazing that anyone would just give away an expenses-paid trip to Israel just because you were Jewish and between the ages of eighteen and twenty-six, but apparently that's what Birthright Israel does. I didn't care what Mamá and Papá thought — when I turned eighteen, I planned to apply for a trip. It was the only way I'd ever be able to afford to see Israel, and Gaby, my best friend halfway across the world.

I'd settled into a routine at school. At least I finally knew my way around and wasn't constantly worried about getting a detention. I kept to myself mostly, because it was hard enough trying to make friends in a language you knew really well and I was still not 100 percent confident with my English. My only real friends were Jon and Rosalia — and Brian, in a way that made me feel strange. It had gotten to the point that one day when I walked into History to find his seat was empty, I felt a wave of disappointment, surprising because I hadn't realized how much I'd been looking forward to seeing him. It's not because I *like* liked him. He was just smart and funny and I enjoyed speaking to him. Okay, yes, and he had really lovely brown eyes, I'll admit that.

Anyway, history class dragged horribly the day Brian wasn't there, and I had to walk to my next class alone.

The hallway was even noisier than usual, and there was a crowd down at the far end. As I got closer, I heard Jon's voice and he sounded distressed, almost like an animal in pain. I pushed my way through the crowd and saw that Derek, Martin, and Trevor had managed to get hold of Jon's notebook and they were playing a game of keep-away. I'd never seen Jon so agitated; his face was bright red and streaked with tears and his fists were clenched. He walked toward Trevor, who taunted him with the notebook.

Just as Jon reached for it, Trevor threw it to Martin.

"GIVE IT TO ME!" Jon shouted. "IT'S PRIVATE!!"

Martin threw it back to Trevor.

"Private, eh?" Trevor taunted. "Let's have a look what Freak Boy here spends so much time scribbling."

I'll admit that I had a burning curiosity to know what Jon wrote in that notebook all the time — but only when he wanted to show me. I didn't want some jerk like Trevor to just barge his way into Jon's innermost thoughts. The look of panic and horror and utter despair on Jon's face when he saw Trevor open the notebook spurred me forward.

"STOP IT!" I shouted, dropping my books and pushing my way through the crowd until I was close enough to Trevor to get my hands on the book. "GIVE IT TO ME!"

"Get lost, *puta*!" he said, trying to yank the book away.

I couldn't believe that this guy who didn't even speak Spanish would use that word, would dare to call me such a thing. I heard people laughing, so it must be a word that a lot of Americans understood. My face was burning with shame and anger, and without even thinking of where I was or the potential consequences, I slapped Trevor hard across the face. Shocked, he let go of the notebook, and I snatched it away from him and clutched it to my chest.

"How DARE you call me that!" I hissed.

I heard gasps and watched in slow motion horror as Trevor raised his hand like he was going to hit me back.

"MR. RICHARDS! I hope you aren't planning to use that fist to hit another student," said Mr. Perez, a teacher from one of the classrooms nearby.

Trevor's hand fell to his side.

My heart was beating so hard I was sure the crowd of gawking, muttering students could hear it.

"Okay, people, time to get to class," Mr. Perez said. He took in Jon's tearstained face, the red mark on Trevor's face, and me, clutching Jon's notebook as if my life depended on it.

"We're going to take a trip down to the principal's office," he said. "NOW."

"It's not my fault, Mr. P!" Trevor complained. "That chick is crazy. *She* hit *me*!"

He made me want to hit him again, even though the teacher was standing right there. How dare he pretend that it was *my* fault, when he was tormenting Jon like that?

Jon was standing with his arms around himself, rocking back and forth and whispering something I couldn't make out. He reminded me of the way Paquito, my late *abuela*'s dog, used to get during a thunderstorm — like he wanted to crawl out of his own skin.

I was afraid to touch Jon in case I upset him more. But his distress was so palpable, it was radiating off him in waves. I put my arm around him and he jumped, but I rubbed his back gently.

"It's okay, Jon. Look, here's your notebook."

I handed it to him. It looked like one of the pages was slightly torn, but otherwise it was in one piece.

His back, which had been as tense as a steel plate, relaxed slightly.

"Th-th-thanks, Dani."

He fingered the cover and I saw his eyes fill with tears again.

"Okay, people, let's go. Principal Williams's office, on the double," ordered Mr. Perez.

My stomach was churning the entire way down to the principal's office. I'd never been in trouble before, ever. I'd never even had a detention. And now I was being sent to the principal's office for hitting someone — even if he *did* deserve it.

Trevor was sent in to see Mr. Williams. Jon and I had to sit outside his office, waiting. I was scared to death that I would be suspended, that I'd be labeled a troublemaker, that I'd end up with even fewer friends than I already had.

"I'll tell him that you did it for me, Dani," Jon said. "I'll tell him it's not your fault."

I didn't want to tell Jon that I'd actually hit Trevor for me. Hitting him felt so good, so right, I wished I could do it again and again and again. It was like all of the unfairness, all of the teasing, all of the humiliation, had been right there in Trevor's taunting smile, and to wipe that look off his face, *BAM!* Well, I only wish I'd hit him harder.

"Thanks for getting my book back," Jon said, opening it and fingering the pages lovingly. "It's . . . very special to me."

He took a pen out of the back pocket of his jeans, turned to a clean page, and started to write.

I'd always tried to give Jon privacy when it came to his notebook, but I couldn't control my curiosity any longer.

Anyway, at that point, I figured I'd earned the right to ask a question or two.

"So, Jon, what exactly do you spend so much time writing in that notebook?"

He was still scribbling away when he answered.

"Letters."

I was about to ask him letters to whom when Principal Williams's door opened and Trevor sauntered out.

"I'll see you next, Mr. Nathanson," Mr. Williams said. "Mr. Richards, please sit down at the other end of the office AWAY from Miss, er . . ."

He looked at me inquiringly. I was tempted to give him someone else's name. It was too bad Jon was Jessica's brother, or I'd have given him hers. "Bensimon. Daniela."

"Keep away from Miss Bensimon, Mr. Richards, if you know what's good for you, until your mother comes to pick you up. I don't want any more trouble from you today."

Oh no. Mother picking up? Please don't let him call my mother. She'll kill me. And when she's finished killing me, my father will take over.

The principal's door closed, leaving me to stew in my anxiety, imagining the various methods of demise my parents were going to devise for me when they found out I was in trouble. Me, Daniela: the responsible, good, never-gets-into-any-trouble daughter. I felt overwhelmed with guilt that I was going to make my mother worry. But then I wondered, *Why* should *I feel guilty?* Standing up for Jon felt so right. Even though my hands were trembling and my stomach was churning with nerves, I didn't regret anything, even slapping Trevor's face. *Especially* slapping Trevor's face.

"He saw the mark on my face where you hit me," Trevor called from across the office. "You're gonna get suspended, you crazy bitch."

"That's enough, Trevor," snapped Mrs. Pierce, the school secretary.

I ignored him, but inside I was seething, and my palm tingled as I replayed how my hand made contact with Trevor's jaw. I never knew I had that sort of violence inside me. It was almost as if slapping him had let something loose inside me, something dark and terrible, and I was afraid it would take me over. I'd always thought of myself as such a good girl, as calm, mild-mannered Daniela. And now . . .

Maybe Trevor was right. Maybe I *was* a little bit crazy.

"My brother, where is he? Is he all right?"

I looked up. It was her, Evil Jessica. *Perfecto.* Just what I needed right now. Maybe I should just slap her face, too, since I was already in trouble. I could just let it all out and get one massive punishment.

But her face wasn't its usual ice shell of cruel perfection. She was worried about her brother.

"Did you see Jon? Is he okay?" she asked me.

"He's with the principal," I told her. "He was very upset, but I think —"

"What happened?" Jessica asked me.

She glanced over at Trevor, who was eyeing her appreciatively. I suspected the feeling was not going to be at all mutual, especially once I told Jessica what he did.

Which I proceeded to do. For once, her cold stare wasn't directed at me — it was aimed at Trevor, who was still giving her a flirtatious glance, the fool.

"How DARE you!" she said, stomping over to where Trevor was sitting. "From now on, you leave my brother ALONE!"

Trevor looked confused.

"What brother? You mean . . . that geekazoid is your *brother*?"

If I'd had the money to wager, I'd have bet that if we weren't right outside the principal's office, Trevor would have been hit in the face for the second time that day. But instead, Jessica just said, "MORON!" and stalked back to where I was sitting.

She perched in the chair next to me.

"Such an asshole," she muttered.

"I hit him."

Jessica sat back in the chair and looked at me. A real look, like she was seeing me, Daniela, for the very first time.

"Seriously? For real?"

"For real. That's why I'm in here, in trouble."

She stuck up her hand to do a high five.

"Good for you!" She glanced over at Mrs. Pierce and whispered, "I wish she wasn't here so *I* could hit the jerk."

"It felt very good," I confessed. "Especially because . . . well, because he was being so horrible to Jon. I couldn't believe all the other kids were just watching it happen without doing anything to stop it."

Jessica's face became hard, masklike. "No, none of those cowards would stick up for Jon against a guy like Trevor."

Her eyes met mine and for once they were warm and almost . . . friendly?

"But you did. Thank you."

She sounded like she really meant it, too.

"Jon's different, you know," she said. "You've probably noticed that."

Was that a trick question?

"Well . . . yes, I have. But . . ."

"He has Asperger's syndrome. He's really smart but he doesn't always get how to interact with people. And kids like Trevor have always picked on him. It makes me want to tear them limb from limb."

So maybe this Asperger's syndrome explained why Jon seemed like *un tipo raro.*

"Is that why he knows so many facts?"

"That's part of it — he's got an incredible memory for

things that he's interested in. And he'll tell you about them whether you're interested in them or not."

"And . . . is this why he didn't understand about 'raining cats and dogs' and your aunt wearing her 'heart on her sleeve'?"

Jess laughed.

"He told you about that? Omigod, Mom was *so* embarrassed! Yeah, that's all part of it, because he tends to be really literal about language. Like when Jon was little, Dad called home from a business trip and asked Jon what he was doing and Jon said, 'I'm talking to you on the phone,' because that's what he was doing right then. He didn't realize Dad meant what was he doing *before* he got on the phone."

So much about Jon made sense once Jess told me this. But at the same time, I couldn't help wondering how she could be so angry about Trevor and all the other kids being mean to her brother when she had been so unkind to me.

Principal Williams's door opened and he walked out, followed by Jon. Jess jumped up and hugged her brother, who looked uncomfortable in her embrace but glad to see her nonetheless.

"Are you okay?" she asked Jon. "Do you need to go to the nurse for some extra meds?"

"I'm okay now," he said, pulling away from her. "I've got my book."

He held it up, looked over at me, and smiled.

"Thank you, Dani."

Principal Williams wasn't looking quite so friendly.

"Miss Nathanson, could you please take your brother back to class? As for you, Miss Bensimon, I'd like to speak with you in my office."

I could almost hear the funeral bells tolling. I could definitely hear Trevor snickering from across the office, the *burro*. I refused to let him see that I was scared to death at the thought of being in trouble, that this was the first time I'd had to go see the principal in my entire life. I squared my shoulders and started to head into Mr. Williams's office, when Jessica stopped me by putting her hand on my arm.

"Hey — I really mean it. Thanks."

There was still a part of me that wanted to say that I didn't do it for her, I did it for Jon. But the better part of me just said, "*De nada*," as I continued into the principal's office to meet my fate.

Chapter Twelve

NORMALLY, I WOULD HAVE BEEN suspended for hitting another student, according to Principal Williams, but since there were "mitigating circumstances" in my case (namely, Trevor being such a complete *idiota*, although he didn't put it in exactly those words), he let me off with a warning. He did, however, call my parents. I begged him not to — I told him that my parents were already under a lot of stress because we'd only recently immigrated and that I'd never been in trouble before and please, couldn't he just give me extra homework or something, but no, he insisted on picking up the phone.

Papá was furious. I could hear his raised voice coming through the receiver from where I was sitting across the desk. I think Principal Williams even felt bad for me when he put down the phone.

"You did the right thing by sticking up for Jon when he was being bullied by another student," he said. "But, in hitting Trevor, you crossed a line. We have a zero-tolerance policy against violence here at Twin Lakes High School — as I said, had there not been other factors involved, you would have been suspended."

I stared down at the floor, unable to meet Mr. Williams's eyes. Whatever rightness I felt about hitting Trevor was gone, replaced with dread about what would face me when I got home.

"Next time, call on a teacher or an administrator for help," Mr. Williams told me, before sending me back to class.

I was suddenly a minor celebrity — "The Girl Who Hit Trevor" — but I wasn't able to enjoy my new social visibility, because I was sick at the thought of having to face my parents.

A snail could have crawled faster than I walked from the bus stop to our apartment. With good reason — Papá was waiting to berate me as soon as I opened the door.

"Brawling at school? My daughter? The disgrace of it! What has happened to you since we came to this country? As bad as things were in Argentina, at least my daughter didn't behave like a common fishwife!"

"But, Papá —"

"Don't *but, Papá* me! Go to your room until Mamá gets home!"

I opened my mouth to protest, but he glared at me so angrily I was afraid he was going to hit me. He wouldn't even give me a chance to explain. Even though I'd always been a good daughter and done the things he and Mamá expected of me, he automatically thought the worst. My eyes filled with angry tears, and in that moment I hated him. I stomped down the hallway to my room and slammed the door as hard as I could, so hard the books fell off my nightstand.

So much emotion was pounding my head and twisting my gut that I felt like I might explode with the force of it. I paced the narrow space between the beds a few times, my hands shaking, until finally I threw myself on the bed and gave in to angry tears. I tried to remember what it felt like to love Papá, to remember the days when it seemed like he loved me, but all I could feel was anger and frustration.

When my sobs calmed down to hiccups, I figured I'd better try to make a start on my homework before Mamá got home, because I knew the rest of the evening would be filled with "discussions" about my behavior and lectures about what a terrible daughter I was.

I'd finished everything except for math when Sarita came bounding in.

"Hi, how was your day? Papá says you're in Big Trouble!"

She leaped onto my bed, crushing my math homework.

"Sari! Careful!"

"Sorry." She shuffled her bottom off my papers and tried to iron the creases with her hands. "But are you? In Big Trouble?"

"In a way, yes. But it wasn't really my fault. And Papá wouldn't listen."

"Like Papá EVER listens."

Sari knew way too much for a kid her age.

Later, when my mother got home, I heard her shout from the kitchen.

"DANIELA! *¡VEN ACÁ!*"

"Guess it's time to get yelled at again," I sighed.

"Wait!" Sarita exclaimed. She ran to her bed and reached under her pillow for the worn, silk-edged scrap of material she slept with.

"Here, take my Baba with you for luck," she said, crushing it into my palm.

I hugged her, trying to ignore the tears that threatened to escape my eyes.

"DANI!"

"That's Papá. I'd better go."

My parents were both sitting stiffly on the worn sofa in the living room. Mamá looked exhausted, and I felt a twinge of guilt that I was another problem for her to carry on her already burdened shoulders. But then anger layered on top of guilt like frosting on a cake. Why should I feel guilty for helping Jon? Would it have been better to have just walked away and done nothing?

"Dani, Papá tells me the principal called and said you hit a boy in school today and that you were almost suspended." She sighed heavily. "I cannot believe this of you, Daniela. We did not raise our daughter to behave this way."

"But, Mamá —"

"*¡Silencio!* Don't interrupt your mother!" Papá shouted.

I clenched my teeth so tightly I got a throbbing pain at the back of my head, but it was the only way I could stop myself from shouting that they were both wrong, that they were being unfair; I had to bite back the question that pounded in my brain: *Why won't you just* listen *to me?*

Mamá was droning on and on about how she was working her fingers to the bone and getting varicose veins in her legs, all so that Sarita and I could have a better life, and would it kill me to stay out of trouble so she could sleep at night without worrying and . . .

The phone rang, cutting off her recitation of all my faults. Mamá got up to answer.

"Yes? This is Daniela's mother. . . . You want to thank her — for what? . . . I see. Yes, she is a fine girl. Yes, her father and I are very proud. Thank you very much for calling, Mrs. . . . Nathanson, yes, it was a pleasure to speak with you, too. Good-bye."

My mother put down the telephone and crossed her arms over her chest.

"Daniela, why didn't you tell us that you intervened to save this boy, Jon Nathanson, from a bully?"

I couldn't believe she was asking me such a ridiculous question, when neither she nor my father would let me tell my side of the story. It was so ludicrous it was almost funny. I clenched Sari's Baba in my fist and the anger and frustration I'd been holding inside me all afternoon burst out.

"Because you wouldn't *listen*! Because every time I tried, you told me to be quiet or to go to my room or not to interrupt. Because you and Papá just assumed the worst about me, even though I've never been in any kind of trouble before at school, ever."

My mother stood there, a stricken look on her face. My father sat on the sofa, staring at the carpet.

"I work so hard to be good at school and good at home. I do my homework and help with Sarita and dinner and try to do as much as I can to help you, Mamá, because . . ."

I couldn't say it. As much as I wanted to name the thing that blanketed our house with misery each and every day, to throw it into the room and force everyone, but mostly my father, to deal with it, I just couldn't.

"Why don't you ever listen to me?" I asked instead. "Why can't you just *trust* me?"

My mother sat down, heavily, on the sofa, and wiped a tear from her eye.

"I'm sorry, *querida*. I'm sorry we didn't give you a chance to explain."

I looked at my father, waiting for him to apologize, but he sat next to my mother, resolutely avoiding my gaze.

I wanted his apology even more than my mother's; I just wanted to hear him say *desculpame*, "I'm sorry," but I knew deep down that all I was going to hear was silence. I swallowed the disappointment, and it lay heavy inside of me.

Chapter Thirteen

TREVOR WAS ABSENT FROM SCHOOL the next day. He was suspended, because it wasn't his first bullying offense. When I walked into Language Arts, Jon was sitting at his desk writing in his notebook as usual, but he looked up and greeted me with a big smile.

"You were awesome for hitting Trevor yesterday," he said. "Thanks."

"I shouldn't have hit him," I said. "But I had to get your notebook back. They shouldn't have taken it."

"No, they shouldn't have," Jon said, closing the cover and stroking the book lovingly. "It's private property."

Someday, I hoped Jon would trust me enough to show me what was in there.

After class we walked down to the cafeteria together for lunch. We were sitting at the table talking about *Hamlet* when Jess walked up. To my astonishment, she sat down with us.

"Hi, I'm Jessica, Jon's twin," she said, as if I didn't already know the identity of my tormentor. She held out her hand for me to shake.

I couldn't believe that after all the scornful looks and nasty comments, she was acting as if we'd never met, like none of it ever happened. I felt like telling her to go away and leave me alone. But then I looked over at Jon, who was sitting there with a big grin on his face. He was innocent of all this and he was my friend. So I took her hand and shook it and said, "I'm Daniela. But you can call me Dani."

"I just wanted to thank you again for standing up for Jon yesterday," Jess said. "You were incredible. I mean, slapping Trevor Richards in the face! I wish I'd been there. Forget that — I wish I'd done it myself! That guy is such a creep, and he's been hassling Jon for years."

I felt like I was in one of those alien films where the person looks exactly the same on the outside, but within that familiar exterior lies some strange being from another galaxy. Except in this case, the strange being was a distinct improvement on the usual Jess. Still, I was uneasy with the sudden change.

"So, Jon said you moved here from South America somewhere," Jess said. "Chile or something."

"Argentina."

"Oh, like, *Don't cry for me, Argentina*?" she sang.

I was really starting to hate that song. I was beginning to hate the very mention of the film *Evita*. No matter what

Principal Williams said, I was tempted to punch the next person who mentioned it to me.

Instead, I somehow managed to lift the corners of my mouth into the semblance of a smile and said, "Something like that."

"So, it must be really different here, huh?" Jess said.

Talk about the Understatement of the Year.

"Yes, you could say that."

"Like, how so?"

How to even begin? How to compare the wide boulevards of Buenos Aires with the suburban streets of Twin Lakes? How to describe the noises and the smells; the silent shuffle of the mothers of *Los Desaparecidos* as they marched every Thursday outside the Casa Rosada in the Plaza de Mayo; the noise of the street protests, the *cacerolazos*? How to tell this girl who seemed to lack nothing about how proud people like my father lost their businesses and ended up begging for food from the church?

I didn't think there were enough words to make Jess understand "how so."

Fortunately, Jon and his encyclopedic knowledge of my native country saved me.

"Well, for one thing, because Argentina is in the Southern Hemisphere, it's summer there when it's winter here," he said.

"Seriously?" Jess asked. "Cool fact, Jon-boy."

She took a bite of apple, and then leaned over and winked at me.

"So, Dani, tell me the truth. What are Argentinean guys like? Are they hot?"

Images of Beto, so vivid and colorful they almost took my breath away, flashed through my brain in a silent montage, and I felt a wave of intense longing crash over me.

"Yes . . . yes, they are . . . hot."

Jess looked at me intently. "Are you okay? You look kinda . . . sad all of a sudden."

I didn't want to talk about Roberto, especially when I hadn't spoken to him, when I hadn't heard his voice saying my name, when I didn't even know if there was still an us, if he was still my *novio*. But Jon and Jessica were looking at me, waiting for an answer.

"I miss my *novio*, my boyfriend. He lives in Miami now. I don't know when I'll be able to see him again. I haven't even spoken to him on the phone since he left Argentina."

"Seriously?" Jess exclaimed. "No wonder you're depressed! We have to change that right away."

She rooted around in her purse, whipped out a cell phone, and flipped it open. "Call him."

"What?"

"Go on! Call him — what's his name anyway?"

"Roberto . . . but . . ."

"Go on, Dani," Jess urged. "Call Roberto. You know you want to."

The cell phone was beckoning to me like the fruit of the Tree of Knowledge. *Don't touch it — you can't pay her back for the cost of the call.* I looked over at Jon, who nodded his head, telling me I should go ahead. *Don't do it! What if you call Roberto and he doesn't want to talk to you? What if he's already found someone else?*

With trembling fingers, I reached out and took the phone from Jess's hand. She grinned.

"There you go, Dani. Just call me Cupid."

"What?"

"Cupid," Jon explained. "In Roman mythology, he was the god of love. You know, the one who shot arrows at people and is always on Valentine's cards — not that I ever get any," he added in an undertone.

I resolved to send Jon a card on Valentine's Day.

"Oh, yes," I said. "*Cupido.* Thank you, Cupid," I told Jess.

Then I went to dial and with a sinking feeling realized that I didn't know Roberto's number. I didn't even know if he had a cell phone. I stared at the keypad, my eyes filling with tears, the disappointment almost crushing me.

"Go on, Dani — what's the matter?"

"I . . . I don't know his number."

I handed Jess back her phone, buried my face in my

hands, and cried. The day before, I would have died rather than cry in front of her, but at that point I didn't care.

Jon patted me on the back awkwardly.

"Don't cry, Dani. We can call information or look it up online or something."

People in the cafeteria were looking at me, and I knew I was making a scene, but I couldn't stop crying. To have that hope, for one brief moment, that I might hear Roberto's voice saying my name, that I might finally be able to speak to him and feel some connection again and then to have it taken away because I didn't know his stupid phone number . . . it made me realize how far apart we really were.

Then I felt Jess's arm around my shoulders.

"Come on, Dani. It'll be okay. We'll get his number, somehow. And when we do, you can borrow my phone and talk to Roberto for as long as you want."

She handed me one of the postage-stamp-sized cafeteria napkins so I could wipe my eyes.

"Seriously. As soon as you get his number, just let me know. It must suck having to move so far away from each other. I bet you really miss him."

Something in the way she said it made me feel like she really understood what it meant to miss someone, and I actually felt a moment of connection with her, something I never would have thought was possible.

"Thanks. That would mean a lot to me. Because I do miss him — very much."

I dabbed my eyes with the tiny napkin, but I knew I always looked awful when I cried.

"Well, I better go. I don't want to be late for my next class."

"Bye, Dani," Jon said. "And remember, Miami is only one thousand, three hundred twenty-five miles from Twin Lakes. Buenos Aires is more like five thousand, three hundred miles, so Roberto is actually only twenty-five percent as far away as he could be."

I never failed to be amazed at how Jon knew such facts, by the encyclopedic knowledge contained in his brain. And I knew in his own way he was being very sweet, trying to make me feel better about Beto's absence. But . . .

Jess rolled her eyes and we both burst out laughing.

"What's so funny?" Jon asked.

"You, brother Jon," Jess said. "You're just funny sometimes, without really meaning to be."

She grinned at me as I walked away.

In the *servicio*, or the "bathroom" as they said in English, which I found puzzling because there was no bathtub, I splashed cool water on my face and tried to make sense of the fact that I'd just sat at a table, had lunch, joked, and even cried in front of Jessica Nathanson, the person who had probably done more to make my life miserable at

Twin Lakes High than any other person. She'd even offered to let me use her cell phone to call Roberto, because she understood that I missed him, and she'd comforted me when I cried.

I'd just locked the door to a stall when I heard the bathroom door open.

". . . saw you and Jon having lunch with that weird girl from Brazil. What's all that about?"

I held my breath, even though they must have realized there was someone in the bathroom because the stall door was closed. My heart started to beat faster because I recognized the voice as Coty's and she was obviously talking about me to Maybe She's Evil After All Jess.

"She's not from Brazil. She's from Argentina."

"Whatever."

"And she's not weird, you know."

I take that back. Maybe she was still Not Quite So Evil.

"She so is, Jess. C'mon, she hardly has any friends and she walks around in all of your old clothes. I mean, doesn't that freak you out just a little bit, seeing her wearing your outfits? It's like she just raided your closet or something."

"It wasn't *her* that raided my closet — it was my mom. I can't blame Dani because Mom goes off on these give-everything-away-to-charity binges whenever she starts getting sad about . . . well, you know."

No, I don't know. What does Jess's mother get sad about?

"I guess. But I still think she's a little weird."

"I don't know. I mean, the girl hit that bullying moron Trevor Richards. She can't be all bad," Jess said. She was one stall over from me and I was afraid she'd recognize my shoes under the wall, but she was too busy talking to Coty to notice.

A toilet flushed and I missed part of what she said next.

". . . if you had to move to a different country where they spoke another language and you didn't know anyone and you were separated from your boyfriend?"

"Mike better not even move across town or I'll kill him!" Coty said. "But if he did, I guess that would suck and I'd feel pretty lonely."

Another toilet flushed and then I heard running water as they washed their hands at the sink.

"Yeah. She doesn't know if she'll ever see him again. And I know how awful *that* is."

Even over the sound of the water pouring out of the taps in the echoing confines of the bathroom, I could hear the feeling in Jessica's voice. I wondered what was behind it.

The bathroom door opened and as they left, I heard Jess tell Coty, "All I'm saying is, maybe we should be a little nicer to her, okay?"

She was definitely Not So Evil After All Jess.

Chapter Fourteen

"So, EVITA, I hear you've got a mean right hook," Brian said as we were walking down the hall after History. "I'm going to have to be careful what I say around you from now on."

I wasn't sure what a "right hook" was, but figured it must have something to do with hitting Trevor. I blushed.

"I'm really not a violent person by nature," I told him. "It's just that Trevor had Jon's notebook and I know how much it means to him and —"

He put his hand on my shoulder. "Relax — I was kidding, okay?"

"Oh . . . okay."

"Yeah, I know you're one of these idealistic types, who fights for the underdog."

"The underdog?"

"The person who's expected to lose in a struggle — like in a Jon-versus-Trevor matchup, Jon would definitely be the underdog."

"I just did it because Jon's my friend and he was so upset — if you'd seen him, Brian, I'm sure you would have done the same."

"I don't know. I'm not as brave as you are, Dani."

I thought of all the things I was afraid of — Papá being depressed forever, Beto finding someone else, bombs blowing up people in my family and planes crashing into buildings, running into Jess in the hallway — although maybe after yesterday, not so much that — and being poor for the rest of my life.

"I think you've got me mistaken for someone else, Mr. GPS. I'm one of the biggest cowards that ever lived."

He stopped outside the door to my next class, where two girls were trying to affix a huge poster to the wall.

"You need a hand?"

"Yeah, thanks," one of them said. "Can you stick those two corners up there?"

"Sure."

He took the poster and tacked the upper edges to the wall, while the girls taped down the lower corners.

"So what's this for?" he asked. "Oh . . . the Winter Wonderland Dance, hmmm . . . I guess I'll have to find myself a date for that."

The girls smiled up at him hopefully, but he was looking straight at me. I blushed and looked away. Just because he was looking at me didn't mean he was going to ask me, but I had a boyfriend. At least I thought I did.

"I'd better get to class," I said, and headed into the classroom before Brian could say anything other than "Bye."

I had to speak to Beto. I decided to go the library that night and IM him or e-mail him to get his phone number and then ask Jessica if I could use her cell phone to call him. She seemed sincere about it, and I was desperate.

It was hard to concentrate on my homework because I was counting down the minutes till after dinner when I could go to the library. When Sarita got home it was even worse, because she was even more of a chatterbox than usual.

"We did square dancing in gym today and it was really fun except sometimes you had to hold hands with boys and some of them had sweaty hands. Do you find that boys have sweaty hands sometimes? Why do some boys have sweaty hands and other boys don't? I don't like it when they have sweaty hands. When I get married, I'm going to make sure the boy I marry doesn't have sweaty hands," she said, seemingly all without taking a breath.

"Well, Beto didn't have sweaty hands," I told her. "Doesn't, I mean."

"How do you know? Did you square dance with him?"

"Um . . . no. We held hands sometimes when we were walking, just like I do with you."

"Oh."

She jumped onto my bed and leaned her chin into her hands.

"So did you and Roberto ever do kissy-face with each other? Because I can't imagine ever kissing a boy. It's disgusting. I know people do it, but *eeeeeeeeeeeewwwwwww!* So did you? Ever kiss?"

How was I supposed to concentrate on my geometry problems with that kind of running commentary? And how was I supposed to answer Sari about kissing?

"Well . . . we . . . I . . . yes, we did. Sometimes."

"*¡Ay, qué asco!* That's horrible. How did you stand it? Didn't it make you want to throw up? I think it would make me want to throw up."

I thought about sitting in the park, under the ombú tree, and of Beto's kisses. How they were anything *but* horrible. How being there with Roberto after school each day was the one thing I looked forward to when everything else was so awful because of the Crisis. How I wished I were there with him now.

"No, Sari. It didn't make me want to throw up. It was . . . nice. Really very pleasant."

She stuck out her tongue and made a disgusted face, and I couldn't help but laugh.

"You'll understand when you're older."

"No, I won't. I'm never going to kiss anyone except for you and Mamá and Papá and Tío Jacobo. And if Mamá and Papá ever let me get a puppy, I'll kiss the puppy."

Privately, I knew two things: 1) that Sari would change her mind eventually and 2) that there was virtually no chance of our parents ever letting her get a puppy. But I was happy to let her think about kissing puppies. Anything to keep her quiet for long enough for me to get my geometry problems finished.

Mamá was exhausted when she got home from work, and she was so grateful that I'd made dinner and organized Sarita's lunch for the next day that she didn't question me too much about going out.

"Take some quarters so you can call Papá to walk you home when you're finished," she said.

Even though the nights were getting darker, I didn't want to face the awkward silence walking home with my father.

"It's okay, Mamá. My friend Rosalia is going to be at the library and her mother will give me a ride home."

It scared me how easily the lie came out of my mouth, and how small was the twinge of guilt that accompanied it.

"Well, I'll see you later, then," Mamá said. She brushed a stray hair out of my face and patted my cheek. *"Gracias, preciosa."*

"De nada," I replied. Suddenly the guilt twinge felt a whole lot bigger, but I stuffed the feeling down and headed out to the library.

* * *

Beto wasn't online when I logged on to MSN, and I felt sick with disappointment. Instead, I composed a long e-mail to Gaby, telling her about how things were going at school (better) and home (the same) and I was just starting to write to her about my anxieties about Beto when I noticed that he'd logged in.

Hola! I typed. What's up?

Not much. What's up with you?

Well, a girl lent me her phone to call you today and I realized I didn't have your phone number.

☹

Exactly. So are you going to give it to me?

Sure. I have my own cell.

He gave me the number and I wrote it in my history notebook.

Thanks. Maybe I'll call you tomorrow.

Cool.

It would be nice to hear your voice.

Me too.

I miss you.

Miss you too.

How are things?

Busy.

What you up to?

School. And football — we're having a great season. I'm the lead scorer in our league.

Maravilloso!

What about you?

Nothing special. School. Helping out at home. The usual.

Made new friends?

Some. You?

Yes. Being on the team is good for that.

I wish we could see each other.

I watched the cursor, waiting for his response. I wanted him to say, "Yes, me too. Maybe I can fly up to New York," even though I knew it was impossible.

Yeah. But not sure how that's going to happen.

I knew it was true. But it wasn't what I wanted to hear.

GTG, Dani. Talk to you soon?

Already? But he just logged on.

I'll try to call you tomorrow. Buenas noches.

Adios!

Even though I had Roberto's phone number, I felt even more depressed as I logged out of MSN. It's not like I expected an IM chat to be the epitome of romance, but there just seemed to be something . . . missing from our "conversation." It occurred to me that he must have had his own cell phone for a while, but hadn't told me, or tried to call me, when calling him would have been the very first thing I would have done if I could have afforded to get one.

Feeling like I had a vise around my heart, I finished up my e-mail to Gaby. I took out the parts about Beto, though.

I was afraid to write about my fears, in case by voicing them in black-and-white pixels on the computer screen, I somehow made them come true.

It was dark when I walked home, and, if I had to admit it, a little frightening in one place where the street light had burned out. Part of me wished I had Papá walking beside me, however silent and uncomfortable it might be.

The next morning at school I felt queasy with anticipation, waiting for the moment until I could ask Jessica if I could borrow her cell phone. What if the day before had just been an aberration, and she'd gone back to being Evil Jess again? What if I spent the whole morning daydreaming of hearing Beto's voice, and she laughed in my face when I asked her?

The minute hand on the clock seemed to be moving through honey, time was passing so slowly.

"Why are you so antsy today, Dani?" Brian asked me after History.

"Antsy? What do you mean?"

"Nervous. Fidgety. You could barely sit still the entire class. And you must have looked at the clock every thirty seconds."

"Oh. No reason."

Brian gave me a skeptical look. "Well, you just looked at the clock again. It's approximately twenty seconds later than the last time you looked."

I gathered up my notebooks and headed for the hallway. Brian followed.

"So, did they have many social activities at your school in Buenos Aires?" he asked.

"What do you mean?"

"I mean, did you have things like . . . I don't know . . . Winter Wonderland Dances, for instance?"

"No, not that sort of thing. I went to a Jewish day school, so we had parties for different Jewish holidays but not just a dance for the sake of having a dance."

"Well, I think it's an important part of your American education to attend a dance just for the sake of having a dance."

He stopped and smiled down at me. "And I'd like to be the one to take you to it."

I felt hot and cold at the same time. He couldn't possibly be asking me this. Not now. Not when I was finally about to talk to Beto after so many months.

"Uh, I take it you don't like the idea. In fact, it looks like it fills you with extreme panic." Brian shrugged and gave me a lopsided smile that didn't quite reach his eyes. "It was just an idea. For your cultural education — not because I have any untoward intentions. Forget I ever mentioned it."

"I'm sorry, Brian, I just . . ."

I couldn't explain to him that all I could think of at that moment was getting through the morning so I could ask Jess if I could borrow her cell phone. I couldn't explain to him that I needed to know how things stood with Roberto before I could even think about going to a dance with him.

"I've got to get to class," I said, and raced off down the hall like a complete and utter coward.

I saw Jess at lunch, but she was with all her friends and I didn't have the courage to go up and ask her in front of them in case she said no.

"Jon," I said, "Do you think you could ask Jess about the phone for me?"

"What about the phone?"

"Remember yesterday she said I could borrow her cell phone to call my boyfriend, Roberto?"

"Yes. Why don't you call him on yours?"

I felt a flush rise up my neck. Since everyone at my school seemed to have a cell phone it was incredibly embarrassing to have to admit it, but . . .

"Because . . . I don't have one."

"Oh. I'd let you use mine but I forgot to charge it last night so I left it at home."

"Well, thanks but, well, I finally got my boyfriend's telephone number in Miami last night, and I'd really like to try to call him today if she'll let me borrow her phone. Do you think she was serious about letting me use it?"

"She said so. Do you want me to go ask her?"

"Would you?"

He got up and went over to where Jess sat with Coty and the rest of her gang. She looked up and smiled at him in a way that I know she would never have done if it had been me. I couldn't hear their conversation, but Jess looked over in my direction — as did all of the other girls — and she smiled and nodded and gave me the thumbs-up. I felt a wave of relief so big it almost brought tears to my eyes, but I could not, no, I would not, start crying in the middle of the cafeteria for the second day in a row.

"Jess says to meet her by the trophy cabinet right after school ends," Jon said when he came back to the table. "She said she'll call our mom and tell her to pick us up half an hour late so you have time to talk. You can take her phone somewhere quiet to call your Roberto."

That's if he still is my Roberto.

If the first half of the day moved slowly, getting through the second half was even worse torture — every second seemed to take a minute, every minute, an hour. I didn't know whether to cheer or cry when the bell finally rang signaling the end of the day. My stomach was churning and I had to force myself to focus on what books I needed to take out of my locker for homework. All I could think of was dialing Roberto's number and hearing his voice. All I could hope was that in half an hour's time I'd feel reassured that he still loved me, that he was still my *novio*, that things were still as they had been between us, even though we were far apart.

When I got to the trophy case, Jess wasn't there. *What if she forgot? This isn't that important to her. She doesn't care if I get to speak to Roberto or not. I'll die if I've gone through the entire day and I don't get to speak to him! I can't —*

"Hey, Dani — sorry I'm late!" Jess said, interrupting my panic spiral. "I got held up speaking to my last period teacher about a project."

"Oh. That's okay," I lied. "I just appreciate you letting me use your phone." At least the last part was heartfelt and true.

"So, why don't we head out by the back of the art department? It's nice and quiet out there. I told Jon to wait out front to keep an eye out for my mom."

"Whatever you think is best."

We started heading toward the art department.

"Are you nervous? Or just excited?"

"Do you want me to be honest?"

"No, I want you to lie," Jess said. "Duh! Of course I want you to be honest!"

"I've been feeling sick with nerves all day. And excitement. Sort of a mixture."

"When was the last time you actually spoke to him? What's his name again?"

"Roberto."

"So, how long has it been since you two actually spoke to each other?"

"It's been almost eleven months. Since he left Argentina last December."

"Wow. That's a really long time. No wonder you're nervous."

No wonder.

Jess pushed open the door to the outside.

"Here's the phone. I'll go sit on the grass over there to give you some privacy. You can just wave when you're done."

I took the phone into my hand. It was still warm from being in Jess's.

"Thanks, Jessica."

"Hey, it's no biggie. Good luck!" she said with a smile, and headed off to the grassy area a little way off.

My fingers were trembling so much it was difficult to press the small buttons on Jess's phone. My heart was thumping in my chest, so hard I wondered if hearts ever broke through rib cages. Roberto's phone started to ring. *What if he's not there? What if I've waited all day and I get his voice mail?*

"Hello?"

It was a girl's voice.

"Hello . . . I . . . I think I might have dialed the wrong number." I read her the number Roberto had given me, just to check.

"No, you've got the right number. Are you looking for Robbie?"

Robbie? Who is Robbie? And what have you done with Roberto?

"I'm looking for Roberto Saban," I said. A lump was rising in my throat that felt like it would cut off my breathing. "He told me this was his cell number."

"Sure, Robbie Saban. This is his cell. He's in the pool right now. I'll call him for you. . . ."

"Wait!"

I was afraid to ask the question, but I had to do it.

"Who . . . who are you?"

"I'm Amber, his girlfriend. Hold on, I'll get him for you."

I heard her calling "*Robbie, phone for you,*" but it seemed like it was coming from underwater. *I'm Amber, his girlfriend. Roberto has a girlfriend.* Another *girlfriend. I thought I was his girlfriend.* I didn't know if I should hang up or if I should hold on and talk to him. I looked up and Jess waved to me from where she was seated over on the grass. She didn't realize that four words — *I'm Amber, his girlfriend* — had just shattered my entire life.

"Hold on, he's coming," Amber said.

I'm going to hang up. I don't want to talk to him. But I do want to talk to him. I want to ask him how. *I want to ask him* why. *I want to ask him why he didn't tell me. I want to ask him how he could tell me he missed me when he was already dating this Amber.*

I heard giggling and "Stop it, you're getting me all wet" and my finger almost pushed the END button but then I heard his voice. *"¡Hola!"*

"Roberto . . ."

There was silence for a few seconds. Then "Dani . . . *hola* . . . wow, it's been so long since I've heard your voice . . . *¿Cómo estás?*"

"Not very well. Why didn't you tell me, Beto? Why?"

"Dani, I'm sorry . . . it's just . . . look, it's hard for me to talk now. I've got your number now and I'll call you back."

"This isn't my number. I don't have a cell. I borrowed this phone from a . . . friend."

"Give me your home number then."

I tried to imagine talking to Beto on the phone in the kitchen with Papá brooding in the living room, listening to every word.

"No. Send me an e-mail. But don't lie to me anymore."

"I've never lied to you, Dani," Roberto sighed. "I just maybe haven't told you the whole truth. I'll e-mail you, I promise. And I'm sorry, Dani. I really am."

"So am I," I told him, and I hung up the phone.

I sat there, frozen, staring at the ground, my thumb on

the END button, feeling like I wanted the world to end then and there. Feeling like maybe the world *had* ended. Roberto had been my talisman, my secret weapon against despair. Knowing that he was somewhere in the world thinking of me made everything seem possible. But now . . . now I had nothing. *Nada.*

"Hey, Dani — is everything okay?"

"Oh. Here's your phone. Thanks for letting me use it. I . . ."

I don't know what to say because my boyfriend has a girlfriend called Amber.

Jess took the phone and touched me gently on the shoulder.

"You look like you just got hit by a bus, Dani. I don't want to pry or anything, but . . . I take it things didn't go so well with Roberto."

I laughed bitterly.

"You could say that. Not so well at all." I hesitated. Did I want to let this girl, who only days ago was Evil Jess, in on my pain? What made me think could I trust her all of a sudden?

But her brown eyes seemed filled with genuine concern and I felt so hurt, so destroyed, and so desperately alone, that I told her.

"You see, his *girlfriend*, Amber, answered his cell phone. The girlfriend I didn't know he had. The girlfriend he never told me about. The girlfriend I still thought *I was*."

"Oh, Dani," Jess said. "You poor thing. That just sucks. I could kill the creep for doing that to you."

There was a lump in my throat, but I couldn't seem to cry. Instead I felt a numbness, a chill, like I was about to start shivering.

"When I asked him why he didn't tell me, he said it was difficult for him to talk . . . probably because *she* was there. He probably never told her anything about me. It's like I never existed for him now that he's 'Robbie.' That's what she's calls him. Robbie."

Jess put her arm around me and gave me a hug. A week before, if you'd told me that I'd be standing outside the art room being hugged by Jessica Nathanson while she consoled me about being dumped by my boyfriend, I'd have questioned your sanity. But there I was in her embrace and it felt far less strange than I'd have imagined.

"It totally sucks and he's a complete jerk for not being honest with you. Seriously. I hate guys who are liars."

"He said he didn't lie — he just didn't tell me the whole truth."

"Yeah, yeah. Whatever. Either way he's a jerk. But the thing is, Dani, it was always going to be hard to keep up a long distance thing, wasn't it? Like did you ever talk about how you were going to do that?"

"He said he would always love me. He said in his IM last night that he missed me."

"But he could miss you and still have a girlfriend. Like

he could miss you and miss Argentina and everything to do with his life there — like with how it was when he was Roberto and all, and he could still love you from a distance, but realize that the likelihood of you guys actually getting to see each other any time soon is pretty minuscule, so he wants someone to hang out with in the meantime because he's a guy, and he's in tenth grade, and it's not like you guys are married or anything."

I heard the sense in what Jess was saying, but part of me hated her for saying it. It was as if she could read my mind.

"Sorry, Dani, I'm sure this is the last thing you want to hear right now. I'll shut up. Just know that if you want to talk or if you need to use my phone to call him to shout at him and tell him that he's a complete asshole or anything like that, I'm here for you, okay?"

She sounded so kind, so sincere, that the lump in my throat finally moved upward and I felt the hot prickle of tears.

"Th-thanks, Jess. For everything."

"Oh, Dani . . . wait . . . here, I've got tissues in my bag."

She rummaged around and handed me a travel pack of tissues. I took one.

"Take the whole pack, just in case. Listen, I have to get out front because Mom's probably waiting for me. Do you need a ride home or anything? I'm sure my mom would love to meet the girl who defended Jon."

I'd missed the bus and Papá would be mad I wasn't home for Sarita, but did I want Jess to see the modest building where we lived? Yet despite all her past meanness about the lunch vouchers and clothes, she was going out of her way to be kind.

"If . . . if it's not too much trouble, I would love a ride home. Thank you."

When I met Mrs. Nathanson, I could see where Jess got her good looks.

"I'm so pleased to meet you, Daniela," she said, as I slid into the backseat. "Thank you so much for sticking up for Jon. It was very brave of you and I know it meant a great deal to him — and to us."

"It wasn't so brave really. It was just wrong what Trevor and his friends were doing. That notebook is really important to Jon."

Jess and her mom laughed.

"Don't we know it!" Mrs. Nathanson said. "We're not allowed to touch it or go near it. What is in that notebook is a constant mystery to everyone in our family. The only people who know are Jon and his therapist."

"And Dad," Jon said.

For some reason I couldn't understand, that caused a complete change of atmosphere in the car. In the rearview mirror, I saw the smile wiped off Mrs. Nathanson's face, and when I looked at Jess her face was closed, masklike.

207

"Well, Daniela, where do you live?" Mrs. Nathanson asked, her voice falsely bright.

I gave her my address.

"So, what's the Winter Wonderland Dance like?" I asked, trying to do my part to ease the tension. "Have you been to it before?"

"I . . . didn't make it last year," Jess said. "But I heard it was fun."

"Well, I was just wondering because . . . well, because someone asked me to go."

"Seriously? Come on, spill! Who?!"

"Do you know Brian Harrison? He's in my history class."

"Brian Harrison . . . tall, brown hair and eyes?"

"Yes, that's him."

"He's kind of cute. So are you going?"

"Well, not exactly. I didn't exactly say no to him — although I think he thinks I did. But I didn't say yes, either, because I was so busy worrying about talking to Roberto and . . . to be honest . . . I was shocked that he'd asked me. It's just now . . . well, now I'm wondering, why not? Why shouldn't I go with him? Maybe it would be fun."

"You should totally go!" Jess said. "It's just what the doctor ordered!"

Jon laughed in the front seat. "That's another expression for you, Dani. *Just what the doctor ordered.*"

I laughed, too, imagining a doctor handing me a prescription with a picture of Brian Harrison and the Winter Wonderland Dance poster. But then a worrying thought hit me.

"So what do people wear to these dances? Is it very fancy?"

"Don't worry about that," Mrs. Nathanson said. "I'm sure Jess could lend you something. You two are the same size. It's the least we could do after you stuck up for Jon."

I glanced over at Jess, remembering the scene on the first day at school, and worried that she'd be angry at her mother for volunteering the loan of her clothing. But she didn't look at all upset.

"Why don't you come and sleep over?" she said. "We can find you something to wear and maybe watch a movie or something?"

Sleep over? At her house? Like I used to do with Gaby? Things were getting more and more strange. It was as if my hitting Trevor and getting dumped by Roberto had transformed the girl from Evil Jess to Fairy Godmother Jess. Or maybe it had transformed me from The Poor Freaky Girl from South America Who Wears Cast-off Clothes to an actual person. A person with feelings.

"Well, I don't know if Brian will still want to go with me. He might have already asked someone else. And I'll have to check with my parents if it's okay. I haven't had any sleepovers since we moved here. But if they say yes, then I'd love to."

At least I think I would.

That night I went to the library and joined a site called Friendster.com that Jess told me about. It was something called a "social networking" site where people put up profiles with their favorite music and films and pictures of themselves and their friends. I felt like a snoop or a jealous girlfriend . . . make that ex-girlfriend . . . but I decided to search to see if Roberto had a profile there. There was nothing under Roberto Saban but then I searched under Robbie Saban and there he was . . . the boyfriend formerly known as Roberto. There he was, complete with pictures of himself surrounded by other tanned kids on a beach. In several pictures he had his arm around a blond, curvy girl in a bikini, who I could only assume was Amber. I wasn't sure why I wanted to torture myself, but I looked at the pictures for an hour while I was supposed to be doing homework. I stared at Amber on my computer screen, trying to figure out what she had that I didn't. What made her so special in Roberto's . . . sorry, *Robbie's* . . . eyes that he'd forgotten about me, about the hours we spent together in the park under the ombú tree, about the dreams we had of traveling the world together.

Sixty minutes of staring revealed nothing other than that 1) she was extremely pretty and 2) she was in Miami when 3) I was not. With a sigh, I logged out of Friendster and turned to my homework. After trying to figure out love, even geometry seemed easy.

Mamá wanted to talk to Mrs. Nathanson, but after she'd had a conversation with her, she said that I could sleep over at Jess's house on Saturday night, a prospect that had me both nervous and excited. But so did something else, something I had to tackle first.

When I got to history class, Brian smiled at me, but without his usual open warmth. There was something uncomfortable between us; I could tell that I'd hurt him.

"Is your offer still open?" I asked him. "About the dance?"

He looked surprised but said, "Uh . . . sure. I haven't found any other girls in need of a cultural education since yesterday afternoon."

I took a deep breath and, feeling my cheeks starting to flush, I said, "Well, I'd be honored to have you attend to my cultural education needs — if you are still willing, that is."

This time, the smile went all the way to his eyes.

"Awesome! That's great. I'll make sure you have a good time . . . and learn a lot about the cultural expressions of the American teenager while you're at it, of course."

"Of course."

Class started, so we couldn't discuss it any more, but Brian kept glancing over at me and smiling. After the hurt of yesterday, after feeling so rejected by Beto, it made me glad that we were going to the dance together.

As he walked me to my next class, Brian asked, "So what made you change your mind? You know, about going to the dance with me."

"Um . . . let's just say that I was letting the past hold me back from taking advantage of all the new experiences that America has to offer, and . . . well, I've come to the realization that it was a mistake. A big mistake."

Brian looked at me intently, and then said softly, "If it was a guy holding you back, he was an idiot to let you go . . . in my humble American opinion."

I blushed and found something very important to stare at on my shoe. But his words made me feel warm inside.

I felt his hand on my arm. "I'll see you tomorrow, okay? And I'm really glad you're going to the dance with me."

Finally getting the courage to look him in the eye, I said, "Me, too."

The next day I was telling Rosalia all about it after ESL. She was going to the dance with her boyfriend, Ricardo, which made me feel better because at least I'd have a friend there.

"Oooh, he's *muy guapo*, that Brian Harrison! What are you going to wear?"

"Well, you know that girl, Jessica Nathanson?"

"You mean 'Evil Jess'?"

"Yeah, well, it turns out she's Not So Evil Jess now. Ever since I stuck up for her brother against that *majadero*, Trevor, she's been really nice to me. And believe it or not, she invited me to go sleep over at her house on Saturday and she's going to lend me one of her dresses to wear to the dance."

"Wow. That's a change from her giving you a hard time every time you wore her castoffs."

"I know. I'm not sure what to make of it. Like part of me is expecting her to start being mean again any minute. But she can be really kind when she wants to be."

"Well, that girl has been through some tough stuff, you know."

"No, I don't know. Like what?"

"You didn't know? *Ay*, her father . . . her father was killed. . . . He was working in the Twin Towers, you know, on 9/11."

"*¡D-os mío!* Seriously? . . . *Oh no . . .*"

I thought of the news reports I watched all the way in Buenos Aires, over and over on the television screen, of the smoke billowing out of the first tower, of the plane hitting the second tower with a fiery smash and then more smoke until they both collapsed, one after the other, pancaking into a cloud of dust, taking so many innocent lives with them. And to think that somewhere, in that huge pillar of dust, was Jess and Jon's father. *Oh my G-d.*

I remembered how devastated I felt when Tía Sara was killed, how sudden it was: One day she was alive and looking forward to the birth of her baby and then she went to work and she was gone. How must it have felt to lose your father like that?

And then I thought about the car the day before, how everything changed when Jon said that his father knew what was in his notebook. How suddenly Jess's face was a stony mask, and Mrs. Nathanson's face lost all animation. Now it all made sense. I knew Jon had Asperger's but did that mean he didn't realize his father was gone? Surely he must.

"Yeah, it was pretty bad when it all happened. They both missed a lot of school right after 9/11. And then when they came back, it was kinda sick. Like some kids who weren't even their friends were trying to be all buddy-buddy because they were like, *Hey, I'm friends with someone whose dad died on 9/11* kind of thing."

"I know. The same thing happened to me when my *tía* Sara died in the AMIA bombing. It made me mad."

"There was one other kid in town who lost a parent on 9/11, over at one of the elementary schools. Still, we were better off than some other towns in New York, or in

Connecticut and New Jersey, where they had more commuters. My aunt works in Greenwich, you know, in Connecticut, and she says it felt like nonstop funerals for a few months. They lost a lot of people. Like parents at practically every school in town."

"I can't believe this. I can't believe I didn't know."

"How would you? You weren't here then. And I get the impression Jess doesn't like to talk about it. And Jon . . . well, he doesn't really talk about much to anyone. Except to you. I've seen that boy talk more to you in however many months you've been here than in the two years I knew him before you came."

"I don't know. I think we just understand each other because we're both *tipos raros*; me, because I'm from somewhere else and him, because he's so different."

"Well, whatever it is, you got him talking all right. And now you're going to sleep over at their house? I hear it's some place. *Una casa grande*."

Hearing that made me nervous, as if I wasn't nervous enough at the thought of spending an entire night with Jessica Nathanson.

"Make sure you take notes so you can tell me all about it on Monday," Rosalia said. "I want to hear *everything*."

Chapter Fifteen

JESS AND MRS. NATHANSON picked me up on Saturday afternoon. When the buzzer rang from downstairs, I grabbed my bag to run down so they wouldn't have to come up and see our tiny apartment, but to my horror and embarrassment, Mamá insisted that they come to the door to meet her and Papá. *Perfecto.* I'd just about convinced Jessica that I wasn't a freak and then she'd meet my family and be convinced I was one again. Plus, she'd see that we live in an apartment the size of a postage stamp and that would be the end of this strange new friendliness she was showing me.

"It's such a pleasure to meet you," Mrs. Nathanson said, shaking Papá's hand. "Daniela is a wonderful girl."

Papá didn't look so convinced, but fortunately, he'd shaved and combed his hair so he looked semipresentable.

"We're very happy to meet you," Mamá told Mrs. Nathanson. "Thank you for having Daniela to your house. She's been lonely since we moved here from Argentina."

Gracias, Mamá. Thank you for making me sound like a complete LOSER with no friends in front of Jess and Mrs. Nathanson. Now can you please STOP TALKING!

"It must have been a difficult transition for all of you," Mrs. Nathanson said.

Just then Sarita came bounding down the hallway to see what was going on.

"¡*Hola!* Who are you? I'm Sarita. Are you Jessica, the one whose clothes Dani got from Jewish Family Services? She was really embarrassed when you saw her wear them, but I think your taste in clothes is *fabuloso.* I wish you were my size so I could wear your clothes, because . . . I . . ."

"Sari! ¡*Cállate la boca!*" I hissed. I swear my family must have been conspiring to see how badly they could embarrass me. I was just waiting for Papá to start shouting about how awful I was to make my humiliation complete, but he'd already retreated to the sofa and the television.

Jessica was cracking up, though, and Mrs. Nathanson was smiling. Sarita never failed to charm.

"Well, now that you've met my family, maybe we should go," I said, anxious to leave before Sarita let any more secrets out through her chattering lips or my mother convinced them that I was a complete loser.

Jess winked at me, like she knew exactly why I was so desperate to get out of there. She didn't realize I was worried that Mamá would invite them in for tea and biscuits, and then they'd see the cramped living room with the worn carpet and the ugly sofa and chairs.

"Well, I wish I had a little sister like you, Sarita," Jess said.

"That's what you think," I muttered under my breath.

"Instead, I'm stuck with a huge, hulking brother. I can't share clothes with him or anything."

"I'm glad I don't have a brother," Sarita said. "My friend Kelly has a brother and he likes frogs and spiders and icky things and sometimes he smells bad. I'm glad I have Dani. She smells good and she reads me stories."

Maybe Sari wasn't so bad after all.

"Well, luckily my brother, Jon, doesn't smell too bad," Jessica told Sari. "Mom has him well trained when it comes to showering and using deodorant."

"Speaking of Jon, we should get going," Mrs. Nathanson said. I wanted to kiss her.

And finally, before Mamá could offer refreshments or Sarita embarrassed me further, we headed downstairs to the car.

The drive to Jess and Jon's house took us through a part of Twin Lakes I'd never seen before — a beautiful, wooded, leafy area of town, where the houses were surrounded by vast tracts of perfect green lawns set behind stone walls topped with white picket fences. And the size of the houses . . . I'd seen *las casas grandes* in Argentina, but these were just enormous.

I wondered if Jess would tell me about her father since I was going to be staying over at her house, or if she just assumed that I knew. It felt awkward knowing what had happened, but being unsure if I could or should talk about it.

When Mrs. Nathanson pulled into the driveway, I realized Jess's house was just as grand as the others in the neighborhood. It was a large, white house with black shutters and an impressive stone entryway. Jess's mom pulled the car into a three-car garage, although there were only two cars parked in it.

I heard a dog barking from inside the house when I opened the car door.

"That's Max," Jess said. "Don't worry about him. He's all bark and no bite."

The door to the house opened and a large golden retriever bounded out to greet us, wagging his tail and jumping up, first on Jess and then on me.

"Down, Maxie! Behave yourself!" Jess commanded.

Max jumped up again.

"As you can see, he's a highly trained animal who obeys our every command," said Mrs. Nathanson.

"Yes, but we love him anyway, don't we, Maxie boy?" crooned Jess.

"Hi, Dani!"

Jon was standing in the doorway, looking much more relaxed than he ever did at school. It was something about his posture. At school, his shoulders were always hunched over in a defensive way, whereas at his home he was standing up straight and just seemed . . . different. Happier. And he wasn't clutching his notebook to his chest like he normally did, either.

"Hi, Jon! It's nice to see you out of Language Arts class and lunch."

"You should come and see the movie theater. Jess, let's show Dani the theater. Maybe we can watch *Star Wars* or something."

"More like 'or something,'" Jess said. "There is no way I'm sitting through *Bore Wars* again. No way, no how."

We walked into a kitchen that looked more like a cathedral than somewhere to make and eat food.

"Wait a minute," I managed to gasp out. "Are you telling me that you have your very own movie theater in this house?"

"Don't freak out, Dani. It's not a full-size movie theater," Jess said matter-of-factly. "It's just a simple home theater."

I don't think she realized that to me there was nothing simple about having any kind of movie theater at home. Home movie luxury at la Casa Bensimon was having a

VCR — and if we were really lucky, maybe sharing a bag of microwave popcorn.

It wasn't like that at Cinema Nathanson. There was a separate room in the basement, complete with eight huge leather chairs that reclined with footrests and had holes in the arms for your drinks and little tray tables for snacks. It was the most luxurious movie theater I'd ever been in.

Jon got me a Diet Coke from a small refrigerator in the corner and Jess made a bowl of popcorn while the two of them argued over what we should watch. They finally agreed on *Back to the Future*, because I hadn't seen it and Jon and Jess both agreed it was a classic.

"This is one of Dad's favorites," Jon said as the movie started.

I glanced over at Jess, and her face had that tight, closed look again. As I was watching the movie there was a part of me imagining Jon and Jess sitting there with their father, Before. Before he got up for work one day and didn't come home again, just like Tía Sara. Before his life was ended by terrorists, just like my aunt.

I couldn't imagine how awful it must feel to be Jess. Because even though it felt as if the *papá* I knew and loved had gone and left a morose, bitter hulk in his place, at least I still hoped that somewhere, underneath his unshaven and depressed exterior, lay my real *papá*. My *papá* from Before. But for Jess there was nothing, nothing but memories.

As soon as the film was over, Mrs. Nathanson told us to come for dinner. She poured herself a glass of chardonnay and asked me questions about life in Argentina. She seemed to know quite a bit about the Crisis — apparently the local United Jewish Federation, of which she appeared to be an active member, made a big fund-raising appeal for their impoverished Jewish brethren. Even from five thousand miles away, we Bensimons were the poor neighbors. I resolved never to tell Papá. He'd probably never let me sleep over again.

We helped clean up the dishes afterward, then Jess said, "Come on, Dani. Let's take your stuff up to my room."

I grabbed my small overnight bag and followed Jess up the wide, polished wood stairs. Her room was amazing. Her bed alone was the size of my entire bedroom, and it was piled high with brightly colored pillows. She had her own flat-screen TV on the wall, and a couple of beanbag chairs in case you didn't want to lounge on the bed to watch it.

Everything was perfectly matched, like it was all chosen by a chichi decorator, from the curtains to the carpet to the throw cushions. Well, everything except for a patchwork quilt at the foot of the bed, which stood out in the otherwise picture-perfect room. It wasn't even a *nice* patchwork quilt — the patches weren't even made from squares of fabrics that went together.

"So, Dani, let's find you something to wear to the dance," Jess said, leading me over to her closet. She threw open the doors and I couldn't help letting out a gasp, because it could have been a small bedroom in itself and it was filled almost to overflowing. She had so many clothes I couldn't believe she ever had to wear anything twice. Even when my father owned a clothing business I didn't have that many clothes. I couldn't believe she even missed that shirt I was wearing on the first day of school.

Jess must have read the expression on my face.

"You know, the reason I freaked out about the shirt you were wearing the first day of school is because it was the last present my dad brought home from a business trip before he . . . well, before 9/11," she said. "He went to some conference in Monaco and brought it back for me. He used to have to travel a lot for his work and he brought back a present from every trip he went on, no matter how short it was, even if it was just overnight. Mom always called them his 'Guilt Gifts.'"

"Jess, until the other day I didn't know . . . about your dad. That he . . . you know . . . well, that he . . . that it was on 9/11 that he . . ."

"Seriously? I thought the whole world knew. It sure felt like that at the time. Like I was in a fishbowl and everyone was looking at me — 'There's that girl whose dad was killed in the World Trade Center.'"

She hugged her arms around herself as if to protect herself from the memory of all those glances.

"But I wasn't here then. I was still in Argentina on 9/11."

"That's true. I guess I feel like even though it's over two years later, everyone still thinks it's the defining part of me — like for the rest of my life I'm always going to be Jess the 9/11 Girl."

"I never thought of you like that. But maybe that's because I didn't know."

"It's weird. Right after it happened, it was all everyone ever wanted to talk about, like, *How do you FEEL, Jess?* I swear, they were like vampires, sucking on my grief, wanting to be a part of it. I mean, I'm sure they felt sad, and all. But they still had their dads coming home from work every night."

She hugged herself even tighter. "And they didn't have to watch their dad dying over and over and over again on TV."

Plane. Fireball. Flames. Collapse. Smoke. Dust. I'd watched it over and over, too, from far away in Buenos Aires. To me they were images, awful images where I knew that people were dying — but it wasn't my father going up in smoke.

"Now everyone just pretends like it never happened — at least to my face. They're too caught up in who Jennifer Aniston is dating or who's going to ask them to the Winter

Wonderland Dance. The people who talk about 9/11 the most are politicians, and that just makes me mad."

Jess walked over to the bookshelf, picked up a snow globe, and handed it to me. "Dad brought this back from a trip to Switzerland."

I shook it, creating an instant blizzard for all the little people in the Alpine village inside.

"The first thing I'd say to him when he'd get home from a business trip was 'What did you bring me?'"

I looked down at the snow settling on the rooftops inside Jessica's snow globe, and thought that maybe she felt some guilt about these gifts, too.

"I'd give all of these things away, every single thing, if he would just walk through that door one more time so I could tell him how much I love him," Jess said. There was a catch in her voice, and when I looked up she was wiping away tears.

If Jess were Gaby, I would have given her a hug, but she wasn't. She was Jessica Nathanson, and I wasn't that kind of friend to her. I wasn't even sure she considered me a real friend at all, or if I was just some sort of charity case that she'd taken on out of gratitude because I stuck up for her brother. In the end, I gave her an awkward pat on the shoulder.

"I'm sure he knew you loved him. That you still love him."

For some reason, this made her cry even harder. *Nice*

work, Dani. You are possibly the world's worst excuse for a grief counselor.

"It's just . . . you don't know . . . nobody knows . . . not even Mom . . ."

She was crying so hard, I couldn't stop myself. I put my arm around her shoulders and gave her a hug.

"What is it, Jess?"

Jess grabbed my arm and looked at me through mascara-ringed eyes. "You have to promise not to tell anyone, ever. You have to swear on something totally sacred that you will never tell."

What could be so awful that she hadn't told anyone, that she needed me to swear on something sacred? The desperation in her eyes frightened me.

"Come on, Dani — swear!"

"Okay . . . I swear . . . I swear on . . . the memory of my *tía* Sara."

She released the death grip on my forearm and reached for the box of tissues on the dresser.

"The thing is, Dani, that morning . . . the morning of September 11, I could have gotten up and had breakfast with my father. He came into my room and said he was toasting me a bagel before he left for work, but I didn't want the carbs and I figured I'd rather have five more minutes of sleep. I thought I'd see him later. I figured I'd have dinner with him that night. Or breakfast the next day. Or the day after. I had no idea that he wouldn't come home . . . that he would be . . ."

I hugged her tighter, because I didn't know what to say. How could my words possibly ease her pain?

"I would have done the same thing, Jess. How could you know the Towers would . . . I mean, no one expected . . . no one could have ever imagined . . ."

I was really, really bad at this. I wondered if there was anyone who was good at it.

"I'm just saying that I'm sure that everyone would have done the same thing you did. We all would have assumed we'd see our dad later and rolled over for an extra few minutes of sleep."

"Not everyone," she sobbed into my shoulder.

"What do you mean?"

"Jon got up. Jon had breakfast with him. Jon got to say good-bye."

And then I understood. As much as she loved Jon and was totally protective of him, he was still her *brother*. It didn't matter if her parents were alive or killed in an awful terrorist attack — the sibling rivalry for their affection continued.

"Jess, come on, you've got to try to stop punishing yourself like this. You'll make yourself ill."

I gave her another hug, and handed her more tissues.

She wiped her eyes, then blew her nose loudly.

"Yeah, and if I don't pull myself together, you'll have to go to the dance in some awful rag and we can't have that, can we?"

"Don't worry about the dress. It doesn't matter. I'm sure I can find something to wear."

"Who are you kidding? It so totally *does* matter. You think Brian Harrison wants to take out Cinderella *before* the makeover by her Fairy Godmother?"

I felt myself blushing when she said Brian's name, which was strange because a few days before I thought I was still in love with Beto. Why was I having such a hard time picturing his face now?

After what seemed like fifty dresses later, we finally settled on a simple strapless dress of pale blue silk ("matches your eyes" according to Jess) and a white cashmere shrug. The cashmere was soft and strokeable, like a kitten's fur. I lay on Jessica's bed cuddling it, surrounded by discarded choices.

"I can't believe a piece of clothing can be this soft." I sighed. "I guess we should put all these other dresses back."

"Yeah, if you don't want to have to sleep on the floor tonight," Jess said.

When the dresses were finally back in the closet, Jess caught me fingering her strange, mismatched quilt.

"A 9/11 group made that for me," she said. "They asked my mom for my dad's clothes so they could make it out of stuff we recognized. That's why it's not color coordinated like a lot of patchwork quilts."

She flopped down on the bed next to me.

"See this blue square? Touch it — feel how soft it is. That was his favorite T-shirt. He wore it practically every Sunday morning when he went to get bagels and the *New York Times*. And see this Hawaiian pattern? He got that shirt when we stayed at the Polynesian Resort at Disney World. He got up onstage and danced at the luau, because he said he might as well get his money's worth out of the shirt and make a complete fool out of himself."

I looked over at the photograph of Jessica's father on her nightstand. He had Jon's curly brown hair and Jess's deep brown eyes, but with laugh lines around them and his mouth, which was open in a wide smile, like someone just told him the funniest joke. His arms were around Jon and Jessica, and everyone looked so . . . happy. I wondered if it was as hard for Jess to look at that picture as it was for me to look at photos of Tía Sara after she died.

"He's wearing that shirt in the photograph, isn't he?"

"Uh-huh. Mom took it on the way back to the hotel room after the luau. Even Jon is smiling and he hardly ever smiles for pictures. That was one of the best vacations ever."

She pointed to a terry cloth diamond. "See this? That was his bathrobe. I used to love when he'd just shaved and he'd kiss me because his cheek was so smooth and he smelled like aftershave."

Jess jumped up and opened the top drawer of her dresser. She rummaged through her underwear and then pulled out a lumpy pair of socks and brought them to the bed. Out fell a bottle of aftershave — Cool Water by Davidoff.

"Here, smell this," she said, unscrewing the cap and holding the bottle under my nose.

I inhaled the scent, which was crisp and clean, and I imagined it on the cheek of the man in the picture. Jess dabbed some on the terry part of the quilt, and sniffed.

"I took this from my parents' bathroom before my mom could throw it out or give it away," she admitted. She replaced the lid tightly and hid the bottle back in the pair of socks. "The first time I opened the bottle I almost keeled over, because it was like . . ."

"The hairbrush," I said, nodding.

"What?"

I took a deep breath and tried to explain.

"My *tía*, um, that's my 'aunt' in Spanish, her name was Sara and she worked as a secretary at AMIA, the Jewish Community Center in Buenos Aires. She was eight months pregnant. The day I turned seven, a terrorist drove a truck loaded with explosives into the building where she worked and . . . well, as you can imagine, it was destroyed and . . . my aunt . . . she was killed."

"Omigod, Dani, I'm so sorry," Jess said, putting a comforting hand on my shoulder. "I had no idea."

"Well, about six months after Tía Sara died, we were over at her apartment helping Tío Jacobo pack up her things. Mamá wanted to keep me occupied, so she gave me a box and told me to put all Tía Sara's makeup and nail polish — and my *tía* Sara loved all that girly stuff so she had a lot of it — into a box." I felt a lump starting in my throat as I told Jess the story, even though it happened such a long time ago. "I was emptying out the bathroom drawer when I found Tía Sara's hairbrush and comb. She had beautiful, long, dark, curly hair, and there were strands of it in the hairbrush. And seeing her hair, still tangled in the bristles of the brush, when she was dead and buried in the ground . . . My mother came in and found me crying and then she started crying and then Tío Jacobo came in and he started crying and all of us ended up sitting on the bathroom floor sobbing because of Tía Sara's hairbrush."

I felt a tear escape the corner of my eye and I swiped it away with the back of my hand. Jess was looking at me with this strange expression on her face. It made me wish I'd kept my mouth shut. But then she took my hand and gave it a squeeze.

"You know, Dani, that's *exactly* what it was like. Like the hairbrush."

She stroked the terry square lovingly, and looked at me with glistening eyes. "I've never had anyone understand it like that before. Like I know Mom must feel these things and be hit by moments like that, but we never *talk* about it. Sometimes I think she's trying so hard to be strong for me and I'm trying so hard to be strong for her . . . and who the hell knows what's going on in Jon's head? Sometimes I wonder if he really understands that Dad's gone forever and he's not coming back."

"It must be so hard for Jon," I said. "For all of you, but especially for Jon, because he seems so . . . concrete about everything. At least with Tía Sara, we knew for sure what had happened to her after twenty-four hours, when they pulled her body from the rubble. But for you there's nothing and . . ."

I stopped, realizing with horror that I'd just uttered words that should never have been spoken. Knowing how hard it had been for Enrique's parents, I'd always wondered how the 9/11 families coped without having a body, without having the certain knowledge of how and where their loved ones died that day. Having to imagine all of the horrible possibilities — smoke or flames or being crushed in the collapse or choosing to jump, ending their life in free fall instead of flames.

"I'm so sorry, Jess. I'm such an *idiota*. I can't believe I —"

"Stop it, Dani. It's okay. Well, not okay, but . . . I mean, thinking about all this makes me want to scream and shout and . . . break things and . . . cry, but the thing is, all my other friends just tiptoe around the subject and me, like we're all supposed to pretend it never happened, and I'm supposed to get on with my life. But it did happen. It happened to my dad, and I don't know if I'm ever going to be able to *get on with my life*."

I might not have been a grief counselor, but I knew one thing was true: "Give yourself time, Jess. It's only been two years."

"Right after it happened, I let myself think that he'd been taken to a hospital somewhere in New Jersey or Brooklyn and he had amnesia from being hit on the head by falling debris," Jess said. She rolled onto her back and stared at the ceiling. "Even though deep down I think I knew he was . . . dead . . . I kept hanging on to the hope that he'd suddenly come back to his senses and one day the doorbell would ring and there he'd be, standing on the doorstep with a bandage around his head."

"It's only natural to hope when you love someone. Papá and Tío Jacobo were down at Pasteur Street waiting and waiting, telling each other stories about people surviving in the voids in the rubble for days after earthquakes. Poor Tío Jacobo — he'd tried to steel himself to the idea that Tía Sara would survive but they might lose the baby but then . . . when they pulled her body from the wreckage and he realized he'd lost both of them . . . *ay*, it was terrible."

Jess looked at me with tears in her eyes. "That's so sad — to lose your wife *and* your baby. Your poor uncle."

"No more sad than to lose your father."

"I gave up hope when Mom got the call from the medical examiner that they'd got a DNA match from a body part. She'd taken down his toothbrush and some strands of hair from his comb."

She gave a bitter laugh. "All that was left of my dad was part of a foot. But I guess that's better than nothing, right?"

It didn't seem a whole lot better than nothing. But if a foot was the difference between the feeling that your father had just vaporized into thin air and knowing for sure that he was dead, I guess maybe it was.

"Right."

We both bent over her quilt and inhaled the fresh, citrus scent. For me, it was just a pleasant smell, but I knew for Jessica it was so much more.

Chapter Sixteen

"Hey, date. Can we talk about the arrangements for the Winter Wonderland Dance?"

I banged my head on the top of my locker.

"Ouch!"

"Watch your head!" Brian said.

"Um. Thanks for the warning," I said, rubbing my forehead.

"Sorry. I didn't mean to cause you grievous bodily harm," he said. "I just wanted to make sure we firm up our plans for our hot date."

"Don't you mean our *exploration of the social habits of the American teenager*?"

"Well, yeah, that, too."

"Why do I get the impression that you're focusing less on the cultural aspects of the dance and more on the date part?"

Brian grinned and made a really pathetic attempt to look innocent.

"Who, me? Mr. American Culture? Perish the thought!"

I just looked at him with a raised eyebrow.

"So," he said. "I was thinking that I could pick you up at seven."

Pick me up. That meant seeing my apartment and meeting my family. Maybe agreeing to go to the dance wasn't such a good idea.

"Oh no," Brian said. "You've got your Cloudy Face on. What's the matter?"

"What do you mean, my Cloudy Face?"

He laughed.

"Your face is like the weather — it's totally changeable and unpredictable. One minute it's all sunny and happy — like it was a few seconds ago — and the next, a cloud has passed over, blotting out your usual radiance, like right now. What crossed your mind to make that happen?"

He chuckled.

"And now your face is turning the shade of Heinz Ketchup . . . uh, maybe I should just shut up."

"Yes. Maybe you should, Mr. Weatherman."

"Let me give you a ride home from school at least," Brian said.

I thought of how angry Papá would be if he saw me getting out of the car of a boy he hadn't met, how it might provoke yet another scene at home.

But then I looked up at Brian's brown eyes and cheerful grin. He had a light sheen of sweat over the sprinkling of freckles on his nose and I just wanted to be in his company for a little longer. It couldn't hurt to get a ride home, could it?

"I suppose getting a ride with you would be better than taking the bus," I said, not wanting to let him know that it was infinitely so.

My pulse hadn't quickened that way for a boy since Argentina. Since Roberto. But Beto was in Miami, and he was going out with Amber.

"Well, come this way, madam," Brian said, "Your limo is parked in the rear lot."

He drove a Subaru with an American flag sticker on the back bumper, and I was amazed when he actually came around to the passenger door and opened it for me. I didn't think American guys did that kind of thing.

"Home, chauffeur!" I joked, when he slid into the driver's seat.

He started the engine and looked at me with a grin. "I'd be happy to drive madam home, but first madam has to tell me where home is, exactly."

I blushed, and not just because he looked so handsome with that crooked grin. Because I was embarrassed for him to see how I lived now, compared to how I used to live in Buenos Aires.

"Maybe I should just take the bus . . . ," I said, my hand reaching for the door handle.

"Don't be silly, they've all left already," he replied, reaching across to stop me.

His face was only inches from mine, and his other hand cupped my cheek, increasing the temperature even more.

"What is it, Dani? What's wrong?"

"I . . . it's just . . ."

I didn't know what to say, how to explain, and his lips were so near. I leaned forward and kissed him. I could hear my father calling me a hussy in my head, but I didn't care, because Brian kissed me back.

"Well, that was a pleasant surprise," he said, when we came up for air. "I take it madam has decided to forswear the bus and stick with her humble chauffeur then?"

"Well, you said all the buses have already left."

Brian fake pouted, then took my hand and was serious.

"What's wrong, Dani? Why were you upset just now before . . . well, before our rather pleasant interlude, which I hope will be repeated in the near future."

I hoped so, too, although I wasn't brave enough to say so in words. I just smiled. But the smile faded quickly, as I tried to figure out how to explain to Brian why I didn't want him to see where I lived.

"Things here are so . . . different for me . . . for my family . . . than they were in Argentina. It's not like we were superrich, like some people around here, but until the Crisis we were respectable. My father owned a business, we lived in a nice apartment in a good neighborhood, and I went to the Jewish day school. My parents gave money to charity. But now . . . now we *are* the charity. I'm wearing the cast-off clothes Jess Nathanson's mother gave away to Jewish Family Services, we live in a tiny apartment that I'm embarrassed for you to drive me home to, and I'm freaked out that you're going to have to come to pick me up in a few weeks' time because you're going to see it. And I hate it. I really, really hate it."

Brian's thumb wiped away the tear that escaped my eye as I was speaking, and he gently pressed my head to his shoulder. I felt myself watering his T-shirt.

"I can't even imagine how hard it must be for you, having to move to a strange country — and as much as I love the U.S. of A., I bet it seems pretty strange to you — and then starting a new school where you have to do everything in a different language and on top of that to have such a change in your standard of living, too."

His hand gently stroked my back. "No wonder you're crying," he said. "I'm not sure I'd be able to get out of bed in the morning, and here you are on track to make honor roll in a foreign language and beating up bullies in the process. Are you sure your name isn't Wonder Woman?"

I emitted a desperately unattractive sound that was part giggle, part sob, and part snort.

"Nice sound effects," Brian said, grinning.

I almost let go another one, but instead, I hit him.

"I might be a lot of things, but Wonder Woman is definitely not one of them."

"I don't know," Brian said, twirling a lock of my hair with his finger. "I think you're pretty wonderful."

He kissed me again and the feeling was mutual.

"Hey, as much as I'd rather stay here and do this, I guess I'd better get you home," he said, looking at his watch. "Better stop the hanky-panky with the chauffeur, eh, madam?"

"What do you mean by 'hanky-panky'?"

He grinned and leaned toward me.

"This."

One lingering kiss later, I reluctantly nodded my agreement.

"Yes, we'd better stop."

"So where is madam's not-exactly-palatial mansion?" he asked as he backed the car out of the space.

"You mean madam's tiny hovel?" I gave him the address.

Brian leaned over to kiss me when he dropped me off, but I pulled away.

"I'm sorry," I told him. "It's not that I don't want to; it's just . . . my dad might be home and . . ."

"You don't want me to end up filled with more holes than Swiss cheese."

My face must have shown my confusion, because I wasn't sure what my father had to do with Brian and cheese.

He laughed. "Your English is so good, sometimes I forget that you might not get some of my more obscure jokes. I meant that I don't want your father coming after me with a shotgun because he thinks I'm up to no good with his daughter."

Shotgun. Bullets. Holes. Swiss cheese. "Oh . . . now I understand. You're quite funny, in your strange American way."

"That's me, Señorita Daniela — your strange American chauffeur. See you tomorrow."

He squeezed my hand and I could see in his eyes that he wished a kiss came with it. I wished it did, too, but there was no way I was going to risk it.

"*Mañana*, Señor Brian."

I was filled with a strange excitement, a lightness that I hadn't felt since Buenos Aires, as I climbed the stairs to our apartment. But with each step, the heaviness crept back over me, smothering me in its shroud of despair. By the time I reached the front door of the apartment, it was as if the magic of Brian's lips touching mine never happened.

I sighed as I turned the key in the lock and pushed the door open. The apartment was dark, except for the flickering light of the television set. I was so sick of it. I hated being in that tiny place with my depressed father in the darkness. I wanted to stay outside with Brian, in the world of light, where everything seemed possible.

The television was turned to Telemundo, the sports channel, and it was really loud. I was surprised the neighbors hadn't called to complain — except they were probably at work, not sitting around feeling sorry for themselves like Papá.

The contrast between how light and hopeful, how — happy — I'd felt at the bottom of the stairs and how suffocatingly miserable I felt the minute I was in my father's presence hit me like a heavy mallet. I hadn't felt that kind of joy in so long, and I was filled with a sudden deep fury that opening the apartment door could end it for me so easily.

The anger swelled up in me, months of unspoken resentment, and it made me crazy — or brave maybe. But the next thing I knew, before I could think enough to tell myself that it was a bad idea, a terribly bad idea, I marched into the living room and turned off the TV. Then I walked over and yanked the curtains open.

My father sat on the sofa, unshaven in sweats and a T-shirt, his eyes blinking in the light.

"What do you think you're doing?" he growled.

"What Mamá should have done months ago," I said, pacing back and forth in front of the television. "I'm telling you to stop sitting on the sofa feeling sorry for yourself and pull yourself together. I'm telling you that you are dragging everyone in this family down and that you should take the advice of that lady from Jewish Family Services and go see a counselor before you take us down even further. Because I can't take it anymore. It's not fair."

"How DARE you speak to me this way! I am your father!"

"So then *act* like my father — not like this miserable, self-pitying, angry person you've been for the last year!"

"I cannot believe you have the nerve to say these things to me, Daniela. You have no idea what I have been through. How I have suffered . . ."

I thought of Jess, smelling her father's cologne to try and conjure up his presence. I thought of her crying and trying not to let her mother hear, and her mother crying and trying not to let Jess hear, of them both trying to be brave for each other but meanwhile suffering so much by themselves. Yet they went on. I thought of Tío Jacobo, who lost everything, his wife, his unborn baby, yet he picked himself up and moved to America and built a new life, even bringing us over once the Crisis hit. He went on.

Yet my father sat in his sweats on the sofa, unshaven, watching television and feeling sorry for himself all day like this dark vortex of negative feeling that threatened to drown us all with him. No. I refused to let it happen. I clung to the lightness, to the desire to live my life with joy, to the memory of Brian's kiss.

"You aren't the only one who has suffered in this world, Papá. My friend Jessica didn't even say good-bye to her father one morning when he left for work because she wanted a few extra minutes' sleep, and then he never came home because he worked in the World Trade Center and the morning she was tired was September 11," I said.

"*Ay . . .*" Papá covered his mouth with his hand. "I didn't know."

"How *could* you know? You've been so wrapped up in yourself, so angry and miserable — you don't ever *listen* to me when I talk anymore. But . . . do you think it's easy for Jess? Or her mom? Or her brother? Jon and Jess get up every morning and go to school, even though I'm sure there are times when they don't want to. And Mrs. Nathanson, she does all this work for charity when I bet there are times she wishes she could just sit at home and cry on the sofa all day."

Papá sat there with his head in his hands. Part of me expected him to get up and start shouting at me, but he seemed strangely quiet and shrunken, almost, like a balloon with a slow air leak. I didn't know what to make of his silence, but I was like a runaway train, speaking with ever-quickening momentum.

"What about Tío Jacobo — are you saying you suffered more than he did? He lost everything! Tía Sara, the baby . . . At least you still have Mamá and Sarita and me, not that we seem to matter to you at all."

I stopped pacing because Papá made a strange sound and when he lifted his head I saw that he was crying. Tears streamed down his grizzled, unshaven cheeks, and his shoulders shook with sobs.

My anger, seething and strong just seconds before, fizzled at the sight of my father's tears. He looked . . . broken, and I couldn't help but think that it was my words that were the final blow that knocked him down and shattered him.

I rushed over and put my arms around him, consumed with guilt.

"Papá, I'm sorry . . . I didn't mean to . . ."

"No, Dani," he sobbed. "You are right . . . everything you say is right. . . ."

"Papá, no . . . I . . ."

"I've been selfish . . . wallowing in my despair . . . leaving everything up to your mother . . . on her shoulders."

His own shoulders were heaving with sobs. It scared me and at the same time filled me with a deep tenderness that began to rinse away some of the anger and bitterness I'd been feeling toward him for the last year.

"Dani, I'm sorry," Papá wept, clutching at my arm.

"My sweet daughter . . . you think that you and Mamá and Sarita don't matter to me . . . but you are everything . . . everything."

By that point, we were both, as Jess would say, in Sobsville. I hugged him close, and then disentangled myself for long enough to find a box of tissues, because we were both in dire need of swabbing.

After Papá blew his nose and I'd wiped the smeared mascara from my eyes, I took a deep breath and an even deeper risk.

"Papá — I think you should call Mrs. Ehrenkranz from Jewish Family Services and see that counselor. Please. Do it for yourself. Do it for Mamá. Do it for me. Do it for all of us. I know you don't believe in that kind of thing, but Jess said it really helped her to talk to someone after . . . you know, after what happened to her dad."

I was waiting for the explosion, the "How dare you!" but it didn't come. I didn't even get the lecture about how psychiatry is all a bunch of mumbo jumbo just so the doctors can make money from people who are depressed. Papá just sighed heavily, and lowered his head into his hands. We sat there in silence for a minute; the only sound the ticking of the clock on top of the bookshelf. I wondered if I'd gone too far.

But then Papá raised his head and looked at me with reddened eyes.

"I give in, Dani. I will call this Mrs. Ehrenkranz and see what she has to say. If she wants me to go to see one of those shrinking head people, I will go. I just . . ." There was a catch in his voice as he continued. "I just want my daughter to be able to look at her father and feel proud instead of ashamed."

I wanted to tell him that I was proud of him, that I wasn't ashamed. But I think he could tell from the way I dropped my gaze that even if I said the words, they wouldn't be true at that moment. But I still loved him, so I rested my head on his shoulder and gave him a hug.

"That's great, Papá. I think it'll make Mamá really happy, too."

I stood up to go start making dinner. "Come to think of it, something else that will make her happy would be if you took a shower and shaved. Maybe put on a clean shirt and some trousers instead of sweats?"

I reached out my hand to him to help him stand up. He took it and kissed it.

"*Gracias, preciosa.*"

My face flushed, and I pulled my hand away. "I better go start dinner."

Mamá couldn't understand what had come over Papá when she arrived home from work and found him setting the table for dinner, dressed in a pressed shirt, his face clean shaven, his hair neatly combed. Sarita eyed him warily, as if wondering, *Who is this strange man in our apartment?*

But the real shock came over the chicken casserole with rice.

"Estela, I called that Mrs. Ehrenkranz today," Papá said. "I have an appointment to see a counselor at Jewish Family Services tomorrow at eleven thirty. She's going to arrange for a translator to be there in case I feel more comfortable speaking in Spanish."

Mamá's fork clattered to the table.

"*¿De verdad?* Really?"

Papá nodded, smiling.

"But you were so against it. . . ."

"Let's just say I had cause to change my mind," Papá said, winking at me.

Mamá looked from Papá to me and back to Papá and suddenly, she burst into tears.

"Oh, Eduardo . . ."

Sarita was freaked out. She'd never seen Mamá lose it so completely. I figured my parents could do with a little time alone, so I told her to take her plate and we'd have a picnic in our bedroom.

She glanced over her shoulder worriedly as we left the kitchen. I turned and saw Papá getting out of his chair to put his arm around my mother and her turning her face into his shoulder and sobbing before I hustled Sarita down the hallway.

"Why is Mamá crying like that?" Sari asked me when we got to our room.

I looked into her sweet, confused little face and wondered how to explain.

"It's complicated," I told her. "But sometimes, people cry when they're happy. And I think Mamá is happy that Papá is going to go see the counselor, so that hopefully he won't always be so grumpy all the time."

"That would be good," she said, taking a bite of chicken casserole. "But you know what?"

"What it is, *chiquita*?"

"Grown-ups are weird, aren't they?"

"Yes, Sarita. Yes, they really are."

Two weeks later, I'd decided that Mrs. Ehrenkranz was a magician instead of a lady who worked for Jewish Family Services. With a wave of her wand — or more likely her cell phone — she'd arranged for Papá to see the counselor, and then the counselor decided he was clinically depressed and needed to see a doctor and arranged that, and the doctor put him on some pills and even managed to convince him that there was no shame in taking them. He was also attending a group that met twice a week called "Transitions." I didn't know if it was because of the pills or the group or the counseling, or maybe it was all three, but Papá was actually getting up and dressed and shaving every morning, and for the last week he'd picked up Sarita from the bus stop and helped her with her homework.

It wasn't like he was suddenly cured and back to being my old *papá*. He was still short-tempered, and after he'd helped Sarita with her homework, he sometimes went to sleep on the sofa. But at least there were signs, glimpses, of the *papá* he once was.

We were in the kitchen and Sarita was complaining about her subtraction problems.

"What did Math say to Science?" Papá asked.

Sari looked at him, puzzled.

"I don't know. Anyway, we're doing math homework, not science."

"Well, what *did* Math say to Science?" I asked as I prepared the rice for dinner.

"*Ay*, have I got problems!" Papá said.

I turned and looked at him and then the two of us started laughing and laughing. I couldn't remember the last time Papá laughed like that, and I certainly couldn't remember when we'd last laughed at a joke together. It wasn't even that funny. Sarita was looking at us like we were crazy: me doubled over at the sink, gasping, "*Ay, have I got problems!*" over and over, and Papá sitting at the table with his deep, rumbling guffaws.

"Have you been drinking?" she asked, her little face a picture of prim disapproval. "You're acting all *loco*."

"No, *amorcita*. Nothing stronger than *agua* for your old *papá*. Your sister Dani and I are just having a little fun."

A little fun. With Papá. It might have been the pills or it might have been the counseling, but it certainly felt like magic.

"Come on, Dani! I'm going to pee in my pants if you don't let me into the bathroom soon! Just let me in! *Pleeeeease!!!!*"

Sari was dancing outside the door, waiting for me to finish getting ready for the Winter Wonderland Dance. I'd showered and dried my hair and was carefully putting on makeup, enough that I looked good — or at least better than my usual self — but not so much that Papá would start throwing a fit and tell me to go wash it off.

I put on my mascara and then figured I'd better let Sarita in or I'd be forced to clean up her puddle. Sure enough, the minute the door opened she made a beeline for the toilet and her face was a picture of relief as she sat.

"Why does it take so long to put on makeup if you look almost exactly the same afterward?" she asked.

Clearly I hadn't achieved the "looking better than my usual self" goal.

"You'll understand when you're older," I told her.

"You say that about *everything*," Sari said with a sigh. "How much older do I have to be before I start understanding things?"

"I don't know, *chiquita*. I've got a long way to go myself before I know it all."

"Wow, that means I'll never understand stuff because you're already pretty old."

"Thanks for the compliment, you little monster!"

Escaping to our bedroom, I put on Jess's blue silk dress, the cashmere shrug, and the pair of high heels that Mamá had found for me at Goodwill. I couldn't decide if I should put my hair up or leave it down. After staring at myself in the small, cracked mirror on the dresser, I decided to leave my hair down, but to risk Papá's wrath by applying a bit more makeup around my eyes.

"Ooh, you look pretty!"

"Even for an old sister?"

"I didn't mean you were old, old, silly! Just older than me, old."

"I know, *querida*. I'm just teasing you."

"I bet Roberto would still want to be your boyfriend if he saw you tonight," Sari said.

"Well, he's not the one taking me to the dance, and it doesn't matter what he thinks anymore," I said. I said it out of bravado, but after the words left my mouth I realized they were true. I didn't wish that Beto were taking me to the dance. It was the thought of seeing Brian Harrison at my front door that filled me with anticipation.

With trembling fingers, I undid the clasp of the silver heart necklace that I hadn't taken off since Beto put it around my neck the day he said good-bye to me in Buenos Aires, and put it in the top drawer of the dresser. Maybe it was time for new beginnings.

Mamá knocked on the door frame. "*¡Guau!* Dani, let me look at you! You look *hermosa*. Eduardo, come see! Actually, Dani, come to the living room to show Papá."

Walking carefully on the high heels, I followed Mamá down the hallway with Sari following me like an eager lady-in-waiting.

Papá just stared when I walked into the living room.

"Aren't you going to say anything? Do I look that bad?"

He shook his head slowly.

"No, *querida*, you look beautiful. I just can't get over what an elegant young woman you are. When I see you dressed up like that . . . well . . . you aren't my little girl anymore."

I will not cry and ruin my mascara. I will not cry and ruin my mascara.

"Even little girls have to grow up sometime," I said, trying to swallow the lump rising in my throat.

"And get OLD," Sari said. "Like Dani. But at least *I'm* still a little girl."

That was one way to get rid of the threat of tears. Sarita opened her mouth and we were all chuckling.

"Now, Papá, the boy who is taking me, Brian Harrison. He's a nice boy, really. So please don't scare him."

"What do you mean, scare him? Why would I scare him?"

"You know, by doing what you do."

"Estela, do you know what Dani's talking about? What, exactly, do I do that's so frightening?"

"*Sí*, Eduardo, I know what Dani means. Don't be an overly protective father. And Dani, I think you should know that your father can't help himself, and that this boy Brian Harrison, if he's a decent boy, should be able to handle your father. Because your father will behave himself, won't you, Eduardo?"

Mamá was wasted on home health care. She should have headed the United Nations.

Papá just grunted but he looked at Mamá with smiling eyes. She touched his cheek — his shaved cheek — and I was feeling the warmth and rare happiness between them when Sarita said, "*¡Puaj!* You're not going to get all mushy, are you? Because that's just disgusting!"

I realized that was another thing she'd have to wait till she was older to understand.

The buzzer rang from downstairs and I felt my heart leap into my throat as I raced to the intercom to let Brian in.

"Be careful," I said, as I pushed the buzzer. I don't know if he heard me.

Sarita insisted on opening the front door, like a miniature butler. Well, a miniature butler who shouted, *"Dani, your boyfriend is here! And I think he's more handsome than Roberto!"* so that by the time the boy who I wasn't even sure was a boyfriend walked into the room, my face was the color of the red stripes in the American flag.

But he took it all in stride. "Hello, Mr. and Mrs. Bensimon, I'm Brian Harrison."

He held out his hand for Papá to shake. I could tell Mamá and Papá were impressed by his manners. As for me, I was taking in how different Brian looked from his normal, everyday self. I was used to seeing him with his rumpled hair in jeans and T-shirts; that night he wore a dark suit with a crisply ironed shirt and silk tie. He looked . . . well, let's just say I was really happy that I'd changed my mind about going to the dance — and not just because I wanted to have new cultural experiences.

"So, you are driving your own car?" Papá asked. "You will not be drinking alcohol while you are driving my daughter?"

"Of course not, sir." Brian took a folded piece of paper out of his jacket pocket. "I've written down my cell phone number, so if you need to reach Dani for any reason you can call," he said.

Mamá took the paper from Brian and nodded approvingly.

"Thank you. That was very thoughtful. Now why don't you two go and have some fun?"

Good idea.

I could see Papá was about to open his mouth so I grabbed my purse and kissed Mamá good-bye. "*¡Adiós!* See you later!"

"Are you going to do kissy stuff with him?" Sari asked.

I wasn't sure whose face reddened more — Papá's, Brian's, or mine.

"We're going to *dance*, Sari," I said. "We're going to *a dance*."

"And they're not going to do this *kissy stuff* if they know what is good for them," Papá growled.

"*Eduardo,*" Mamá warned.

"Good night, all," Brian called out. "I'll have her home before she turns into a pumpkin."

I saw the confused look on my father's face. It took me a few seconds, too, if I'm honest.

"Cinderella, Papá. Leave the dance by midnight?"

"Oh. I see," Papá said, although I'm pretty sure he didn't.

Brian's lips were pressed together like he was trying hard not to laugh.

"See you later!" I said, beating a hasty retreat for the front hall and escape.

I couldn't look Brian in the eyes because I was so embarrassed by my family, but I was acutely aware of him. He was wearing aftershave, something warm and spicy, and I was watching the way his suit fit his shoulders as I followed him down the stairs.

The cool night air felt soothing to my face when he held the building door open for me, and then he took my hand and walked with me to the passenger door of his car.

He was unlocking the door when suddenly he snorted.

"Kissy stuff! Good Lord!"

I wasn't sure whether to laugh or cringe as he helped me into the car.

"I'm so sorry, Brian. My little sister is . . . well, she's just Sarita, and you can't shut her up."

He walked around and sat in the driver's seat. Then he leaned over to me.

"Well, I was wondering the same thing, actually." His lips were inches from mine. "If we were going to do any, you know . . . *kissy stuff*."

I thought he was going to kiss me, but then he burst out laughing. I ended up giggling pretty hard myself.

"Maybe," I told him. "If you play your cards right."

Jon taught me that expression when I stayed over at the Nathansons', and I could tell I'd used it in the right context by the smile on Brian's face.

I couldn't believe how much effort had gone into decorating the gymnasium — there were murals of snow scenes on the walls and fake snow made from cotton scattered on the tables. Silver and white snowflakes hung from the ceiling, and there were clusters of matching silver and white balloons everywhere. I felt like I was in the dance scene of a Hollywood movie instead of my own life. Maybe it was because I knew I was Cinderella — I was at the dance in borrowed clothes with a handsome prince, but really, I didn't belong there. The thought made me want to run — or stumble, which was probably the best I could do in those heels — but Brian had my hand held tight in his, and then Rosalia spotted us.

"*Hola*, Dani! *¿Cómo estás?*"

I introduced her to Brian and then we went to get some cider. Brian was chatting with Rosalia and her boyfriend when Jess came over. She looked amazing, even more beautiful than usual.

"Hey, Dani, you look fabulous."

"Thanks to you."

"Hey, I'm happy to take some Fairy Godmother credit, but I didn't make you gorgeous to begin with, girl. I just helped with the accessories."

She flitted off to socialize with her friends. The DJ was trying to get things moving on the dance floor, and I realized I had no idea if Brian danced or not. He didn't leave me in suspense for long.

"Come on, Dani. Drink up that cider because I want to see how Argentinean girls shake their groove things."

"Shake their *whats*?"

He just laughed, took the glass out of my hand, and put it on the table.

"Come on. Let's boogie."

There was that "boogie" word again, the one Jake used on the first day of school. It must mean more than one thing. I wondered if English would ever make sense to me.

Brian was a good dancer. My feet hurt from the high heels, but I didn't care. I couldn't remember the last time I felt so happy. Before the Crisis. Before Papá's depression. Before Beto left. I didn't want the clock to strike twelve. I wanted the moment to last forever.

But it didn't, of course. The music always ends. It wasn't because it was late, though. The DJ announced that the principal wanted to say a few words.

Principal Williams took the microphone and made a short speech about how proud he was of the dance committee and how happy he was that everyone was having such a good and well-behaved time. Then he introduced Valerie Hoskins, the head of the student council.

"As you know, the money raised from the Winter

Wonderland Dance is always donated to a good cause," she said. "Given the tragic events of two years ago, and especially how they affected our own community, we felt that this year's proceeds should go to the Families of September 11."

She looked right at Jess when she said it, and everyone in the gym followed her gaze. Jess had that tight look on her face, the same look she had whenever there was any mention of her dad, except for that one time we talked in her room. She forced a smile and nodded her head as a few people started clapping, and then more joined in, until the whole gym was filled with thunderous applause.

I wonder if as happy as she was that the money was going to such a good cause, if she was finding it hard to be Jess the 9/11 Girl again, when she was out having fun and trying to forget about it all.

The minute the lights dimmed and the DJ started again, I saw Jess head for the gym door.

"Excuse me a minute, Brian," I said, and I headed after her.

I found her in the bathroom, locked in a stall.

"Jess. It's me, Dani."

"Yeah." Her voice sounded watery, like she was crying but trying to sound like she wasn't. "Can't a girl even go to the bathroom in peace?"

"I know that was hard, Jess. I mean it's great what

they're doing, but . . . did it feel like the vampires were out again?"

The stall door opened, and Jess came out, red-eyed, holding a piece of toilet paper to her nose.

"You remember that?"

"Of course. How could I forget?"

I put my arms out and she fell into them, crying. "I didn't come to the dance last year because it was too soon after Dad died. But this year I thought . . . I thought it would be different. All I wanted to do was come out and have a good time. To try and be normal again. To be like everyone else and pretend, just for one night, that it didn't happen," she sobbed. "And then, when I least expect it, it's there. I'll never be able to be normal, will I?"

I wished I knew what to tell her. But it's not like I even knew what it meant to be normal.

"I feel guilty for being upset and angry, because it's great they're doing something for the families," Jess sniffed. "A lot of them aren't as well fixed as we are. But . . ."

"But why now? Why tonight? Why can't you just go to the dance and be Jess Nathanson instead of Jess the 9/11 Girl?"

"You understand, Dani. Not like . . ."

The bathroom door opened and Coty came in. She looked at me strangely, and I dropped my arms from around Jess, even though it felt like the wrong thing to do.

"Jess! I was looking all over for you! Are you okay? You poor thing . . . you must be so moved that they are donating all that money in memory of your dad. . . . I was getting all teary eyed myself when Valerie first announced it. Come on, I brought my purse because I figured you might need some makeup repair."

She moved between us and put her arm around Jess, drawing her closer to the sink so they could begin facial repairs.

"Thanks, Coty, yeah, I look like one of the zombies from the "Thriller" video."

Coty opened her purse and started taking out makeup, and I caught Jess's eye in the mirror.

"I'm going to get back to the dance, since you're in good hands," I said.

She mouthed "thanks," but the message she gave me with her eyes went way deeper than that.

I found Brian talking to Jake near the bleachers, just as the DJ announced he was going to play a slow song.

"Perfect timing, Ms. Bensimon," he said. "May I have the honor of this dance?"

I smiled and gave him my hand. Then he led me onto the dance floor and took me into his arms. His cologne smelled comforting and exciting at the same time, and I rested my head on his shoulder and breathed him in.

"That's a heavy sigh. Is Jess okay?"

"She will be," I said. "That announcement came as a shock to her. And then with everyone looking and watching for her reaction . . ."

"Yeah, it can't be easy."

He drew me closer and lifted my chin with his fingers.

"And how are you, Dani? Do you feel like you are getting the full American cultural experience?"

I shook my head no. He looked puzzled.

"My American cultural experience is distinctly lacking in *kissy stuff*."

He laughed softly, and then bent his head toward me.

"I think we can rectify that."

And he did. Rather nicely.

"So did you have a good time at the dance?" Jon asked me at lunch the following Monday.

"Oh yes. It was wonderful," I told him. "How come you didn't come?"

He looked away from me, obviously uncomfortable.

"Too many people. I don't like the noise." And then, looking down at his food, he muttered, "And who would go with me anyway?"

I felt bad for him.

"Come on, Jon, I'm sure someone would go with you, if you asked them. I would have gone with you if Brian hadn't asked me first."

He looked at me, amazed. "You would have?"

"Why do you sound so surprised? We're friends, aren't we?"

"Well, yes, but . . . there's a difference between having lunch in the cafeteria and going to a dance."

"Only that I'd be wearing high heels so I'd be taller. And my feet would hurt more. Oh, and I'd be wearing more makeup. And a dress. Probably borrowed from your sister, but a dress, nonetheless."

"And I would have had to wear a suit and a tie, which I hate. That's another reason for staying home and watching movies and writing in my notebook."

"But honestly, Jon, when you saw Jess getting ready to go out, didn't it bother you one little bit that you weren't going, too?" I asked him.

"You sound like my mom," Jon said. "And my therapist."

"Ouch. Well, I don't mean to. But seriously. Didn't you wish you were going one tiny little bit?"

"I don't know. Kind of. But I still think I probably had a much better time at home with my movies and my notebook."

I felt sad for Jon. It seemed like he was missing out on so much. But I couldn't tell if he was sad for himself or if he was content with things the way they were. Maybe I shouldn't judge how things were for him by the way I'd want them for myself. Still . . . I wouldn't have missed the experience of going to the dance with Brian for anything.

"You know, everyone always tells me I should talk to people more instead of spending so much time writing in my notebook," Jon complained. "But I *like* to write in my notebook. My notebook doesn't get sad and cry and go to its room. It just *is*."

Where did that come from? I was *really* wondering what he wrote in there. I took a deep breath and finally got up the nerve to ask him.

"What *do* you write in your notebook, Jon?" I asked. "I mean, you don't have to tell me if you don't want to. It's really none of my business. I guess I'm just curious, since we're friends."

"*Curiosity killed the cat!*" Jon said, smiling.

I laughed. "That's right. I suppose that means you'd better start making my funeral preparations."

Then I cursed myself for talking about funerals. *¡Idiota!* Like Jon needed to be reminded of death.

"I'm sorry, Jon. I didn't mean to joke about death like that."

"Don't worry, Dani," he said with a grin. "It's *water under the bridge.*"

I smiled back, weakly, because I still felt terrible. Like I'd *put my foot in my mouth*. A sudden image of Brian taking off his shoe and pretending to put it in his mouth flashed in my mind.

"I could show you if you want," Jon said. "The note-book, I mean."

A thrill of excitement shot through me at the thought of finally seeing what was in those pages. But at the same time I knew that whatever was in there was deeply personal for Jon, and I didn't want him to feel like I was prying.

"Would you? Are you sure? Only if you . . . you know, feel comfortable having me see it."

"You're my friend, Dani. I trust you," Jon said. And he handed me the notebook.

I wiped my hands on a napkin and carefully opened to the first page. I wasn't sure what I expected to see, but I know it wasn't this:

Dear Dad,

Today it is three months and four days since 9/11. This is my second notebook. They still haven't found you yet. Jess and Mom keep hoping you are alive but I've watched the collapse of 2 World Trade Center over and over on TV, watched the floors collapse into each other and then the huge cloud of dust. I know that as much as Jess and Mom hope, there is no way anyone could survive that. It would be statistically impossible, so it's illogical for them to hope. I try to tell them, Dad, but they just get mad at me. Jess starts screaming and crying and yesterday she called me a cold-hearted bas-tard. She came into my room and apologized later. More crying. Dad, I think we've used more tissues in the last three months than we used in the previous three years. And that's including the cold and hay fever seasons.

I just want them to find some small part of you, some proof that you were there and now you're gone, so that Jess will stop thinking you are in a hospital in New Jersey somewhere suffering from amnesia and Mom will finally let us have a funeral for you.

I miss you, Dad.

Love, Jon

I felt my eyes begin to water as I turned the page. The entire notebook was filled with letters to his father.

Dear Dad,

Mom got a call that they found you today. Well, that they'd identified part of you through your DNA to be precise. Your foot. Not even your whole foot. Part of your foot. But it's enough. Enough to convince Jess and Mom that you really are gone.

I thought I would feel happier about this. Maybe happy is the wrong word. I thought I would feel more relieved. That now we can finally have a funeral, that Mom and Jess will finally stop hoping that a miracle will happen and you'll walk in the door. But instead I feel terrible. Even though I knew you were gone, now that it's official, it's like we lost you all over again.

I miss you, Dad.
Love, Jon

There were sketches of the Towers, and of Jess, and her Mom, and of teachers and kids at school. Some of the entries were short, but still . . .

Dear Dad,

I miss your pancakes. Mom's don't taste the same. And I miss going to the bagel store with you on Sunday morning while everyone else was still in bed and it was just you and me and we talked about stuff in the papers.

Love, Jon

All that time, everyone thought Jon didn't understand what had happened to his father. All that time, everyone thought that because he wasn't crying like his mother or acting out like Jess, because he seemed so emotionless about the whole thing, that he wasn't feeling the same pain as everyone else.

Well, everyone was wrong, so very wrong. As I turned the pages of Jon's notebook, tears streamed down my face, because in each letter, even the simple *"Dear Dad — I miss you. Mom isn't the same anymore. Love, Jon,"* I felt his loss.

"I should have known you would cry," he said. "Everyone always cries."

"I'm sorry," I said, wiping my tears away with my arm. "I didn't mean to start crying . . . it's just . . ."

I wasn't sure what to say, but I knew I needed to say something, and I had to try not to sniffle while I was doing it, because crying seemed to make Jon uncomfortable.

"It's just beautiful, what you've written," I told him. "It really touched me. Here." I pointed to my heart. "Did you ever show this to your mother or Jessica?"

Jon shook his head so vigorously I was afraid his glasses would fall off.

"Maybe you should, someday. I think it would touch their hearts, too."

"Maybe. A long way away someday," he said, but he looked doubtful.

"Well, thank you for showing me. It means a lot to me."

"You're my friend."

I thought about how we were both strangers in our own ways — me, because I was from another country so I thought and spoke differently, and Jon because his Asperger's syndrome sometimes made him seem like he was. It was because we were both different that we became friends, and because we were different that I defended him from Trevor and became friends with Jess. And now he'd given me this gift of trust, allowing me to see those letters to his dead father, letters he hadn't even shown to Jess or his mother.

"Yes, Jon," I said, putting my hand on his shoulder briefly, because I knew he didn't like being touched, but I wanted reach out to him somehow. "We are friends. Good friends. And that makes me very happy."

A week after the dance, I was doing homework at the library when I got an e-mail from Roberto.

Hola *Dani,*

I expect you hate me by now, and I don't blame you if you do. I just want you to know that I never meant to hurt you. What we had in Buenos Aires will always be special and if it weren't for the Crisis and us having to move so far away from each other, maybe we'd still be together. Or maybe not. We're both young and who knows what the future holds?

But I do know this, Dani. You're a very special girl, and I'll always consider you my friend. I hope, sometime, when you are less angry with me, that you'll consider me your friend, too.

Beto

I was still angry with him for not telling me sooner about Amber, for letting me believe that we were still an "us" when we weren't. I understood that I was the girl he loved, the girl he still cared about when he was Beto. It had been almost a year since we said good-bye, and now he was

Robbie — that part of him had moved on to new things. American things. Things like Amber.

If I was honest, I'd moved on, too. Brian was sitting at the carrel across from me, and when I looked up from my computer his eyes met mine and I felt a rush of warmth seeing him smile. But I would write back to Roberto. Because there was a part of me, the Buenos Aires Dani part, who would always love him and miss him and want to be his friend, the same way I loved and missed Gaby. He was a part of my old life, a memory to be looked back on and treasured.

Brian and I were creating something new.

Chapter Seventeen

PAPÁ PRACTICALLY BOUNCED in the door when he came back from Jewish Family Services on Friday. He had a bouquet of chrysanthemums, bright red, wrapped in fancy paper. "For your mother," he said. "Make sure you set the table nice for Shabbat."

When Mamá came home, carrying two bags of groceries, her eyes widened at the sight of the flowers in the vase on the table next to the Shabbat candles.

"What's this, Dani?" she asked me.

"I don't know. Ask Papá."

"Eduardo?" Mamá called to the living room. "What's going on?"

Papá came in and took the grocery bags from her.

"Go sit down and relax for a few minutes. I'll tell you over dinner."

I finished making the potatoes and took the chicken out of the oven, but all the time I was wondering what mystery Papá was going to reveal while we were eating it.

Finally, Mamá lit the candles to welcome the Sabbath. For the first time in months, Papá started to sing "*Aishes Chayil*."

"*A woman of worth who can find? For her price is far above rubies. The heart of her husband trusteth in her, and he shall have no lack of gain. . . . Strength and dignity are her clothing and she laugheth at the time to come. . . . Her children rise up and call her blessed; her husband also, and he praiseth her, saying: Many daughters have done worthily but thou excellest them all.*"

I saw Mamá's eyes shining with tears. Whatever Papá was going to tell her, it wouldn't be a greater gift to her than this.

After we'd said the blessings over the wine and bread, and everyone was served, Mamá said, "Eduardo, please. What is it that you're going to tell us? The suspense is killing me!"

Papá put down his knife and smiled.

"I have a new job, of sorts. Now don't get all excited, Estela, it's not a paying one yet. But starting next week, I'm going to be mentoring relatives of 9/11 victims."

"Mentoring?" Sari said. "What's that?"

"Talking to them and listening to them and trying to help them get through the grief and the anger about what happened."

"That's wonderful, Papá," I said. "But . . . why you?" I couldn't help thinking that it wasn't that long ago he lay morose and unshaven on the sofa, watching television for most of the day.

Mamá gave me a quieting look as if to ask how I could bring this up now, when Papá appeared finally to have turned a corner. But Papá just looked at me gravely and replied, "I wondered that, too, Dani. Even now, I wonder who am I, Eduardo Bensimon, to think that I could do anything to help these people who have lost so much in such an awful way. But I have lived through this, too. I lost my sister to terrorists suddenly, violently, and unexpectedly. I went through the waiting, the not knowing, the hope of finding her alive, and the despair of knowing that she was really dead. I've lived with the rage at the terrorists for taking innocent lives, and the anger at my own government for not doing more to stop them."

Mamá took his hand and squeezed it, as if to give him the strength to go on.

Papá smiled at her, tenderly, looking so much like my old *papá*, it made my heart turn over.

"These people I talk to, Dani, they are going through the same thing. July 18, 1994, or September 11, 2001 — Buenos Aires or New York City, a truck bomb or a plane, it is the same. Terrorists shattering innocent lives, and the relatives trying to piece their lives back together afterward."

"I'm proud of you, Eduardo," Mamá said. "It's a wonderful thing you're doing."

"Me too, Papá," I told him. I meant it, too.

"Well, I'm just happy you aren't so mean and grumpy anymore," Sarita said. "I didn't like it when you shouted at us all the time."

A few weeks before I would have been afraid of that setting Papá off, but he just laughed and ruffled Sari's curls.

They say that the spirit of G-d, the Shechinah, rests in your home on Shabbat. That night, for the first time in as long as I could remember, it really felt that way.

A few weeks later, I went to the library to work on my *Hamlet* paper. Before I got started, I decided to send an e-mail to Gaby.

Hola *Gaby!*

I miss you, chica! So *much has happened lately, I don't even know where to start. Well, I guess the headline news is that Roberto is no longer my* novio. He *now calls himself "Robbie" and has a girlfriend named Amber. But I'm okay with it. Honestly. No lies. Maybe that's because — newsflash number 2 — I guess you could say I have a new* novio *myself. His name is Brian, and he's* muy guapo. But *more than that, he's smart and funny and I really enjoy being around him.*

I've made more friends here, too. Even that one girl, Jess, who I started off hating, has ended up being a friend. It's strange, isn't it, how sometimes you end up having more in common with the person who you thought you couldn't stand than with anyone else around. . . .

Every day I start to feel a little less like an extranjera *and a little more like an* americana. *Is it the same for you in Israel?*

Things are finally better at home, too. Papá is doing much better. He is working with relatives of 9/11 victims and he said that helping others is making him feel better about himself. All I know is that even though things aren't perfect, at least there are times where I see flashes of my old papá, *and that makes me happy. Maybe as time goes on, those flashes will happen more and more often, until the depressed and angry* papá *is just a bad memory. I hope so, because I've missed my old* papá. *And you know who else I miss — YOU!!*

Sometimes, when I think of Buenos Aires, it feels like a dream. I was born there and lived there most of my life, but now everything is so different, it's hard to imagine I was ever there.

But we were there, weren't we? And we were best friends. And even if I make new friends, you and I will have that special bond forever. You know things about me that no one here knows, and we share so much history. Like to you, 7/18 means something — it's not just another day.

"Hey, Dani!"

I looked up and Jon was standing there.

"Hi, Jon. I'm supposed to be working on my *Hamlet* paper, but I'm e-mailing my friend Gaby in Israel instead."

"Did you know that Israel is only eighty-five miles wide at its widest point?"

I had to deflect Jon before he regaled me with his encyclopedic knowledge of Israel statistics.

"That's amazing, Jon. Are you working on your *Hamlet* paper, too?"

"Yes. Can I sit at this carrel?"

"Sure."

He sat down, and the first thing he pulled out of his backpack was the notebook, the one filled with letters to his father.

"I showed it to my mom and Jess," he said.

"Your notebook? Seriously?"

He nodded, meeting my eyes for a brief instant before looking back down at the pages.

"What did they say?"

"They cried, just like you," Jon said. "But then Mom hugged me and told me how much she loves me and we all sat around, Mom, Jess, and me, and talked about Dad and how much we miss him. Mom got out the photo albums and then we watched the video of Dad doing the hula at the luau when we were at Disney World and we laughed so hard it made my stomach hurt. It was the most we've laughed since . . . well, since it happened. Jess said we need to do it more often."

I smiled at him, thinking about how good it felt when Papá and I shared laughter again over that silly math joke.

"I think Jess is right about that," I told him. "I'm really glad you decided to show them."

"Yeah. I am, too, I guess."

He glanced down at his watch.

"Well, I better work on my paper. Mom and Jess are shopping and they're going to pick me up in an hour."

He pulled *Hamlet* out of his backpack and settled down to work.

I looked back at the computer screen, at the e-mail to Gaby.

Like to you, 7/18 means something — it's not just another day.

And I realized that while that specific date, July 18, might not have the same significance to Brian, or Rosalia, or Jon, or Jess; after September 11 they certainly knew what it meant. Whether it was 7/18 or 9/11, we all knew what it felt like to have our innocence shattered by a terrorist act. We all knew that there was a Before, which we could never return to, and an After, where we had to learn to find joy again.

Because with joy, we overcome the terror. With love, strength, and hope, we prevail.

Acknowledgments

All the wonderful folks at Scholastic Press deserve a horn of plenty filled with *pasteles* and many bottles of Malbec for all the hard work they put into my books: wonder editors Jen Rees and David Levithan, Samantha Wolfert, Tracy van Straaten, Becky Terhune, Adrienne Vrettos, Stephanie Anderson, Jenna Zark, and everyone in sales and marketing and out in the field.

A big plate of homemade *alfajores* to superagent Jodi Reamer for her advice and counsel and for taking care of the tough stuff so I don't have to.

A huge plate of *medialunas* to my critique group, led by the priceless Diana Klemin and including my writing comrades Bill Buschel, Steve Fondillier, Susan Warner, Gay Morris, Tom Mellana, and Alan Schulman, for their invaluable feedback, always given with love and humor.

A big bowl of *arroz con leche* to Ximena Diego, Malaine Miller, and Laura Sanchez for helping someone who'd taken one year of college Spanish back when dinosaurs roamed the Earth sound like she actually knew the language.

A kosher Argentinean steak barbecue with Sarah's special secret marinade to my loving and supportive family: Susan and Stanley Darer, John Darer, Anne Darer and Mark Davis, and the Super D's, Dylan and Daniel. Thanks particularly to Dad, for getting me interested in foreign affairs at an early age and broadening my view of the world. הבה מה טוב ומה נעים, שבח אחים גם יחד

All the delicacies above *plus* a case of the finest Malbec, not to mention my endless love and gratitude, to Hank Eskin for all the times he's talked me down from the ceiling when I've been freaking out about one thing or another, and for his unfailing — and probably misplaced — confidence that I will be featured on *Oprah* someday.

Last, but certainly not least, all of the delicious yummies above, minus the wine, but *plus* a homemade chocolate cake, endless hugs and kisses, *and* a big apology to my beloved children, Joshua and Amie, for all the times I've been grumpy and stressed out because of a revision deadline, or started staring off into space while they've been talking to me because I've suddenly figured out a plot issue. I love you both more than dark chocolate (!!!!) and promise not to sing "Bohemian Rhapsody" in front of your friends.

About the Author

Sarah Darer Littman's widely praised first novel, *Confessions of a Closet Catholic*, won the 2006 Sydney Taylor Book Award. She is also the author of *Purge*. The author lives in Connecticut with her family, in a house that never seems to have enough bookshelves, and loves *dulce de leche*.

2/16   9   9/14